THE NIGHT RIDER ‡

THE NIGHT RIDER

A Novel by Tom Ingram

Bradbury Press   Scarsdale, New York

Ing

1 2 3 4 5   75 76 77 78 79

The text of this book is set in 12 pt. Garamond.

For Marie   ‡

CONTENTS ⌘

1 ‡ *The Trout*

The horse was galloping down the valley, racing urgently toward her, the hoofbeats growing louder and louder, coming closer and closer, drumming the earth. The horse stumbled, slipping on gravel, staggered, flew on at the same frantic pace, then without warning stopped.

Outside, in the darkness under the walnut trees, there was a thickening shadow.

Laura lay in bed stretched motionless with fear. A solitary figure was out there, deep against the first light of dawn. A hand reached out from under the black branches. It was open, beckoning, imploring her for help.

Sudden as lightning the horse and its rider sprang out from the sheltering trees straight toward her. A second more and the window would shatter. The glass rattled. She never saw the rider's face.

Laura shook her head, wondering if she was dreaming or awake. Her eyes frantically searched the yard and the grass under the three walnut trees and the gray meadows falling to the straggle of woods edging the river, where a skein of mist threaded the branches.

There were no hoofprints, no dark patches on the grass made by a galloping horse.

The horse sounded so real, she thought, *I almost knew its name.* But the grass was covered with an unbroken sheen of dew. She glanced quickly around her room. She could just make out the greeny luminous hands on her alarm clock. It was half-past four.

Night was slipping away and under a thin sky the mountains jutted up black and savage. She could see the forest on the other side of the valley. It was dark and impenetrable; light only touched its surface. Laura pressed her forehead against the window and listened intently. She desperately wanted to hear a horse galloping in the distance. She could not forget the open, beckoning hand.

The valley was drowned in silence. There was not even a sound from the others in the house: her brother, James, sleeping in the room next to hers, or her mother and her stepfather, Julian, in their room on the second floor.

Half-past four, I'll never get to sleep again, she told herself. *That's the first time I've had a dream since we came to live in France.* She gazed into the valley slowly resolving in the dawn. She could see one of the wire fence lines dividing the meadow. *I've never seen daybreak in these mountains,* she thought, *a few weeks ago I didn't even know this house existed.*

Suddenly, with heartbreaking clarity, she saw her real

father's face and heard his voice. They were fishing together the day before he was killed. "We'll go out at dawn one day, Laura, it's much the best time even if you don't catch anything."

They never went fishing at dawn. Within a few hours her father was dead, smashed up in a car. Now, two years later her mother had given her a stepfather, an art dealer with an office in Geneva.

"I'll go to the river now," she said passionately.

She dressed quickly in a thick sweater and cord trousers and hurriedly combed her sandy red hair with her fingers before putting on an old canvas jacket. She unhooked her rod and her fishing bag from a wooden peg beside the door.

As she went through the living room, she noticed that the fire, which James had lit the night before, was out. In the foothills of the Alps, where they lived now, the evenings were cold even though it was nearly June.

She crammed her feet into rubber boots, eased back the bolts on the front door and escaped into the morning.

The air stung her nostrils it was so clean and cold. Everything was skimmed of color and eerie. The yard in front of the house merged into the meadow in light which blurred edges and obscured details like the shimmering face of water hiding weeds and fishes in a river.

For a moment Laura half expected to hear hoofs flailing toward her and see the spectral rider who had sheltered under the walnut trees. There was just the waiting valley and the faint sound of swiftly moving water.

She looked up at the house, which was very old and had once been a farm. It crouched against the hillside, pressing itself into the earth for shelter. The walls were heavy

s of pine weathered to the color of plug tobacco. The
ows were small and there were shutters to keep out
w... er. Wide eaves projected far beyond the line of the
walls. Farther up the hillside was a barn now used as a
garage and workshop.

Laura shivered and walked across the yard; then she was
swishing through long grass.

She started to run, a spray of dew flicking off her toes.
She was flying down to the river like a bird swooping low
over the grass which was becoming alive as the gray light
was washed away by the dawn. Her skin was cold and the
air she snatched into her lungs was like icy water.

When she came to the straggle of woods she stopped to
get her breath and looked back. All the way down the hillside her feet had made a line of dark patches in the dew.

She remembered the sound of the galloping horse. The
more she thought about it the more it became a portent.
The valley seemed to be waiting, almost as if the horse and
rider which had wakened her were a sign which it had long
expected.

Laura brushed a strand of hair from her cheek and
turned resolutely into the trees to forget the nagging fear
lurking in the sound of hoofs. At last, through a fringe of
ash leaves, she saw the river which she was growing to
love. A little bird stood wobbling on a stone. No other
living thing was there. Nothing. Just a little bird. Thank-
fully she stepped out from the shelter of the trees.

The river fell between two huge boulders into a long
misty pool. The opposite bank was a low cliff broken by a
gap where a stream trickled out, but on her side a wide
margin was chockablock with boulders. Some were veined
with white, others were shot with lines of green. They

were all sizes, big ones like cars, little ones like refrigerators. The spaces between were filled with pebbles.

Laura flopped down on a boulder and pulled the split cane rod her father had given her out of its case. She fixed on the reel and passed the line through the rings. Then she opened the green plastic box holding her fishing flies, delicately moving them about with a fingertip while she decided which ones to tie onto the line. She chose a Butcher for the point and a Pheasant Tail for the dropper. She picked up the rod and scrambled toward the river.

"Oh, for an almighty great trout," Laura said as she steadied herself on a rock.

She pulled line off the reel, flicked the rod back, checked her forearm and let the rod throw the line forward. She made three casts, each time pulling more line off the reel till she was able to drop the flies into the grape-colored water under the cliff.

On her next cast she screwed up her eyes to catch the faint speck of the Butcher touching the water.

The river split open as a great trout came flashing to the surface; the fly vanished into his mouth, the water closed in a swirl.

The line snapped on Laura's finger. The rod was bucking in her hand as the fish hurled his lashing strength against the hook tearing his lip.

"He's huge! He must weigh pounds!" she shouted to the trees.

Her hands trembled as she felt the fish diving, thrusting himself against the hard, resisting water. Her heart raced and she was deaf to the sound of the river, blind to everything except the quivering rod and the line taut as a piano wire.

"Don't let him break the cast! Don't let him get away!"

Everything was happening so quickly. Everything was so unexpected. The fish was so much larger than any fish she had hooked before. Laura was in a blur—of water, the straining rod, the line cutting through the river.

For an instant the pull of the fish eased and Laura frantically wound line onto the reel.

"I've got you," she cried triumphantly.

The fish threw a flurry of water into the air and darted toward her. Laura let the rod sweep sideways to follow his path.

Now she could see him dark beneath the glittering surface of the river. He was twisting, jerking against the pain of the hook.

She reeled in fast. Abruptly the line stopped. The rod was bowed by a lifeless weight. The fish had snagged the line and torn himself free.

As Laura gazed disconsolately at the river, the fish leapt defiantly, his deep flank curved by the strength tossing him into the air. Three times he leapt to show his scorn for Laura, and each time she heard the crack as his body hit the water. When he dived after his last arching leap she saw the derisive flick of his tail as he swam into the deep slicks at the head of the pool.

"He must have been a four pounder," Laura said furiously. "James will never believe me."

The fish had been hooked for such a short time, just a few seconds, and already she couldn't remember everything as it happened. She looked at her hand. The palm was still white where her tense grip on the rod had driven out the blood.

I can't just stand here like a dope, she thought, *the line must be snagged on some stupid piece of wood stuck between rocks on the bottom.*

The line cut into the water about two meters from the bank near a square stone with a white band dividing it almost exactly in half.

She put the rod down and climbed over the rocks till she was standing on this white-banded stone.

"It can't be all that deep—below the top of my boots, with luck."

Laura put one leg into the river. Immediately her boot flattened hard against her calf. She pushed her foot down fast trying to wedge it on the river bed. Stones rocked treacherously and the cold was unbearable. Each time she lifted a foot the current tried to tear it away.

At last the line was fluttering just out of reach. She tried to catch it, bent too far forward and her boots filled with icy water turning her socks into a freezing mush clinging to her toes.

She took one more shuffling step sideways and caught the line.

"Hell's teeth and damnation!" she said under her breath. "My feet are soaked, so I might as well get my arm soaked too."

She moved quickly, thrusting her hand deep under the water. Her fingers touched a hard, curved shape.

"Got it!"

The snag was wedged between two big stones but she didn't feel the slimy velvet which always coats wood which has lain under water for a long time. This snag was smooth and it would not budge.

"What on earth is it? I'll have to stop a minute it's so cold."

Laura straightened up and shook her arms to make them warm. She blew on her fingers which were puffy and the color of beetroot. The sleeve of her sweater and her jacket clung soggily to her arm.

Again she pushed her hand into the water and gripped the snag. She pulled this way and that but it remained obstinately still.

"Blast you!" she said and gave the snag a vicious tug in a different direction. It moved, grudgingly, tearingly, like a loose tooth twisted out of a jaw.

"I'll try that again."

She gave a sudden pull. The snag jerked free and Laura fell in a great splash of icy water. She gripped the snag tight and gulped air as she struggled to her feet. Her hair was sticking to her face and water trickled into her mouth and ran down her spine. She scrambled onto the white-banded rock, shaking herself like a dog.

Then she looked at the snag.

2 ‡ *Winter Meeting*

The snag was a metal ring about four inches across, the color of brass, not polished, but dulled by thousands of tiny scratches.

Laura turned the ring over and began unravelling the line.

Must be one of those old curtain rings, she thought, *the lousy thing made me lose that fish.*

Then she remembered a brass candlestick she had bought in a junk shop. The brass had been covered in a sticky film of verdigris which had taken her hours to polish away. This ring was not tarnished at all.

"Can it be?"

Her hands were shaking as she sensed the weight of the ring. It was so heavy it couldn't be brass.

A great wave of wonderful, laughing excitement surged through Laura, washing away all the disappointment of a few minutes ago.

"It's gold! It must be! It's a bracelet."

She gazed delightedly at the bracelet as she turned it slowly around. It was so oddly shaped—one part was made of three twisted strands, then it grew thicker and swelled into a round boss. *What's it meant to be,* she thought, *it's so worn.*

Three strands twisted together like straws.

Her heart gave a jump.

"Of course! It's three ears of wheat. No wonder I couldn't see what they were. It's like those tests when you find pictures in ink blots. What's this bit?"

Her fingers traced the plaited stalks as she tried to make sense of the round boss held by the ears of wheat.

It was exactly like finding pictures in ink blots, because quite suddenly she saw a face. An angry savage face with bulging eyes and high cheekbones. The hair was thick and swept back over the skull. The chin was hidden by a curling beard writhing into the wheat. Sightless golden eyes stared into emptiness.

"God, he looks fierce. Why did they make him so ugly?"

She rested her hands on her knees and let her head fall forward. The bracelet was so beautiful, yet so frightening.

"Why me?" she asked herself. "Why did I find it? I've never even won a raffle."

A drop of water from Laura's hair fell onto the golden eyes and lay there, then like a tear it slipped down the cruel golden face into her cupped hands.

The eyes blinked, moved. They were staring at her

sharply, cruelly. She tried to tear her gaze away, to move her hands and cover the piercing eyes. Fear swept up her spine. She was gripped by golden eyes staring unflinchingly into hers. She could see nothing else. The world was contracting to a circle of blackness. The trees were fading as a cloud of blackness swept around her. She tried to cry out but she could not speak. She couldn't move. She knew only blackness and golden eyes drawing her down, falling away from her, falling faster and faster, till they were quenched in blackness and she was alone, terrified, hanging in a void.

Her mind was pricking. It hurt as if rough hands were stroking the soft tissue of her brain. Her head filled with thoughts which were not hers.

For an instant she could remember her brother's voice, then it was drowned in a hubbub of voices she had never heard before. She wanted to batter her fists against her forehead to drive out the stranger walking about in her brain, switching off her thoughts, holding her arms rigid against her will.

Suddenly she was shivering and her nostrils tingled with the sharp blue cold of snow. The blackness thinned, dissolved like a mist and she could see.

She tried to cry out. It was no longer summer. The trees were winter trees with snow lying on black boughs. The cliff was hidden by a hard shell of ice. Snow had drifted between the boulders.

There was something rough and hairy under her right hand. She looked at her hand. It was like a copy of hers but paler, narrower, and it lay on the hogged mane of a pony. She forced herself to look down at her body. She was wearing a long dress of heavy brown cloth, belted around her waist. Her toes were curling in soft leather boots, and she was standing ankle deep in snow.

Who am I? She could hear her voice coming from a long way off. *Who am I?*

Then she saw him. A man on a horse standing close to the river's edge. She was overwhelmed by him. He was young, fierce like a brilliant eagle caught by winter beside the desolate river. His hair was a fiery red and he wore a cloak threaded with gold. His left hand rested on the hilt of a sword. She was dazzled by glinting memories of his voice and his face in autumn, in the spring, in hayfields, by roaring fires.

She tried to remember his name. She could feel it forming and dissolving, half-heard sounds in a mind in which she didn't know where to look for an answer. It was like searching for a pebble at the bottom of a cloudy pool.

Five men on horseback were waiting behind him. Each carried a sword under a rough coat of sheepskin. She could hear the mutter of voices as they talked among themselves. One of the men dismounted and stood gazing at the river while he swung his arms across his chest to warm himself.

The pony stirred, shifting its hoofs on the frozen snow. Instinctively she tightened her grip on the reins in her left hand.

All at once her tongue was pushed abruptly against her teeth. She was being made to speak. She was being forced to call out a word. The complicated muscles in her mouth and throat flexed and moved and she spoke.

"Loen," she called and her will snapped and she knew happiness like sun thawing the cold as warm love drove out strangeness and fear.

Laura surrendered, and Laura was hidden within all the

memories and knowledge of another girl, a girl torn between excitement and dread at what was going to happen on the frozen river bank.

"Loen," she called to the man in the golden cloak. "How long must we wait?"

Loen glanced around at her, and their eyes met. She never wanted to be without Loen. She wished she could run her fingers through his hair and feel the warmth of his skin.

"Just a little longer. Tural will come soon."

She had never seen Tural. His name frightened her. It was always spoken in a whisper. She stood close to the pony to share the warmth of its body. The snow bled cold into her feet and her fingers were aching and stiff.

All at once she noticed that the man who had been swinging his arms was standing with his head cocked, listening. He was called Sethor. He was pointing across the river and calling in a low voice, "I can hear them. Two horses."

Loen swung his horse around slowly so its hoofs wouldn't clatter on the rocks.

"Into the trees," he said softly. "Go quietly. You'd better mount, Merta. We may have to ride suddenly."

She put her foot into the stirrup and swung herself into the saddle.

They moved cautiously into the belt of trees fringing the river.

Now she could hear horses moving slowly down the mountain on the other side. She strained her eyes for a sight of the riders coming toward her. Tural, the man whose name she had been taught to fear, was moving through the forest.

Loen slipped his sword in its scabbard and Sethor drew his and laid it across his saddle.

Her skin began to tingle. She saw a movement in the forest.

"Loen! There they are!"

He held up his hand to silence her.

Two horses were picking their way cautiously down the mountain. She couldn't see the riders clearly because the trees grew so closely together. One of the horses slipped and she heard the slithering skitter of its hoofs. The horses and riders were like shadows moving between the trees. Then they were hidden by a fold in the ground and she listened, every muscle tensed as she heard them move invisibly toward the river bank.

She glanced at the men leaning slightly forward in their saddles and then back at the river.

There they were. Two men on horses at the gap in the cliff. Two men so different from each other she couldn't understand why they were riding together.

She heard Loen whisper, "There he is. There's Tural on the first horse."

Tural's hair was so pale it was almost colorless, and his face had the gray pallor of drifts of snow in June. He wore a cloak like Loen's but the color was dark, the golden threads lines of fire on a night sky. He was peering intently up and down the river making sure it was safe to cross. Then he turned to the man riding the horse behind him and she saw the rope. It ran from Tural's hand to the other man's wrists which were tied tightly over each other and then bound to the saddlebow.

This man was bent forward over his horse's neck, a prisoner. His clothes were weather-beaten and torn. A ragged sheepskin was hunched around his neck. His face was sallow with the cold and locks of black hair hung around his sunken cheeks. The horse he rode was a skeleton. She could see its ribs and the sag in its back bending beneath the weight of the rider and two bulging saddlebags of patched and stained leather.

The rope dragged tight as Tural kicked his horse into the river. He kept glancing to left and right. She realized he trusted no one, was always on a knife edge, was always expecting attack.

She couldn't take her eyes from Tural's face. She had to stare at his harsh mouth, at his hair neither white nor flaxen, at the snake-hard body sheltered by the black cloak.

The horses floundered across the river. Tural had almost reached the bank when Loen gently touched the reins, making his horse move forward a pace.

She held her breath. Tural wrenched his horse around. For a moment he stayed motionless. His eyes were counting the men behind Loen before they swept across her skin. Then his head moved slowly up and down acknowledging her and he smiled. She felt the hair on the nape of her neck rise as Tural's red lips drew back from icy teeth.

Tural's horse splashed across the remaining stretch of river and climbed out onto the snowy rocks.

She wanted to gallop away through the trees, do anything which would make her forget Tural's face. But gesturing to his men Loen rode out to meet Tural.

"So you came, Loen." Tural's voice was strangely sweet; it rang cloying in her ears and she shook her head violently to make herself deaf to its numbing tone.

"Is this the man?" Loen pointed at the rider on the gaunt horse. "What do you want for him?"

"Nothing," Tural said, tugging the rope to make the other horse draw level with his own.

She saw Loen's back stiffen.

"You—give the man away? Don't you take gold for your slaves, Tural?"

"You don't keep slaves, Loen." Tural's voice was filled with contempt. "But you need a goldsmith. He's called Arne."

She looked again at the sallow face and the lank black hair of the man tied by a rope to his saddle.

Loen glanced at her making sure she was safe. She heard him say, "Why should I trust you, Tural? You've always hated me, envied everything I have."

Tural cannily scratched his cheek with a white finger.

"I'm still your step-brother, Loen." His voice was soft and persuasive. "How can a goldsmith harm you?"

"Your mother killed my father. Can I forget that?" Loen's voice was hard, unforgiving.

"You drove us both out." Tural made a gesture implying how unjust Loen had been.

"Your mother deserved a strangling. I spared her."

Loen controlled his horse. It was trying to back away from Tural. Its haunches were tense, its head tossing.

"She still remembers you, Loen. When I found this goldsmith wandering lost in the mountains and took him to her, she said, 'Take him to Loen, perhaps the man's skill will make Loen forgive what I did!' "

She saw Loen's hand clench the hilt of his sword.

"I must pay you." He spoke abruptly. "I can't take your gift, Tural. I'll never forgive you and your mother."

The goldsmith was ignoring both Loen and Tural. He sat with his body bent forward, his thin shoulders shaking with the cold. He was quite resigned to being handed to Loen like a block of wood. She heard Tural say, "You can only pay by giving back what we lost."

"What you forfeited." Loen almost shouted.

Tural was staring at her. He bent his head forward slightly and smiled at her again. She shuddered and tried to tear her eyes from his face.

"You'll pay me, Loen. One day you'll find you've paid everything you owe us."

Tural laughed and threw the end of the rope to Sethor.

"Let me touch your hand, Loen," he paused and added scornfully, "my brother."

Tural rode forward and held out his sword hand. It was empty, innocent. His arm seemed harmless, the wrist supple, the elbow bent.

Suddenly a dagger glinted, rose, whipped down in a vicious left-handed thrust at Loen's back.

Her mouth was torn open by a wounding scream. Hoofs stamped. There was a whirl of horses and Loen threw up his arm wheeling his horse aside. She saw the dagger slash through the uplifted folds of Loen's cloak. Her pony was bucking, shying away from the fury of men and whinnying horses and the whistle of swords torn from their scabbards.

Loen reared his horse, its front hoofs flailing at Tural's head. But Tural spun away, his spurs cutting bloody rivers. He smashed through the circle closing around him and leapt his horse into the river. A great wave of gray water rose around him as he thrashed his way to the other side.

In a daze she saw him turn and wave his hand mockingly at Loen and heard him call across the river, "You will pay me, Loen. You will pay me when I come to you."

Then Tural was gone, hidden in the trees and she was throwing herself out of the saddle and running toward Loen with tears pouring down her face as he cried out again and again. "Are you hurt, Loen? Are you hurt?"

But she couldn't reach Loen, to touch his back and know if he was wounded. He was hidden from her by a black mist. For a moment she heard him call out, "Merta." His voice was a long way off. Then she heard nothing, she was lost in blackness lit only by one point of light which grew and became a golden face. The darkness thinned. She could see and hear. She was watching the first rays of the newly risen sun shining on the bracelet and listening to the sound of the river and the leaves stirring on the trees.

Her name was Laura.

"But—who was I?" Her voice cracked against the rushing water and the trees.

Laura gazed into the golden face on the bracelet. The bulging eyes stared uncaringly into emptiness.

"I was called Merta!" Her hands clenched the bracelet. She stood up and slid the gold the fish had given her into the pocket of her jacket.

3 ‡ Julian

Laura was so lost in thought as she walked the last few paces up to the house that she didn't see Julian lurking in the shadow of the half-open front door.

"Laura! Where the devil have you been?" Her stepfather's voice was like a hammer shattering glass.

Laura stopped dead, her eyes staring wildly at Julian, hardly believing what she saw.

He was poised to rush down on her; one hand seemed raised to strike. His dark eyes were narrowed and accusing, his lean body tense with anger.

She took one slow, hesitant step toward him.

"Fishing." *What have I done wrong,* she thought, *why's he so angry with me?*

Julian's hand fell quivering to his side.

"You're soaking wet. What happened?"

"I fell in."

"You might have drowned," Julian said reproachfully. "Don't you ever think about your mother?"

"Of course I . . ." Laura stopped. Julian's words hurt. "I just got wet, that's all."

"Tell me when you go down to the river, understand!" Julian was almost screaming. "Didn't she suffer enough when your father died?"

Why did you say that? Laura's mind spun, *didn't we all suffer then?* She wanted to say, "Do you think I'm made of wood, do you think I can't feel," but she said simply, "I can't if you're asleep."

"Stay indoors, then. You're not running heaven knows where, risking your neck, just to catch fish."

How can I tell him what it was like, she thought, *does he enjoy hurting me? I can't stand any more.*

She walked purposefully toward the door, her eyes fixed on the ground. Julian stood aside to let Laura pass. For a moment she thought he was going to catch her arm and fill her ears with more unjust bitter words. Then she was past, safe in the living room. She had dreaded touching Julian. She looked quickly over her shoulder. Julian was staring across the valley, his shoulders slumped forward. Laura hurried to her room.

She automatically hung up her fishing bag and rod and kicked off her rubber boots. Her socks made dark stains on the floor.

She sat down and pulled the bracelet out of her jacket pocket and put it on the table. Instantly she forgot Julian.

"What happened?" she whispered.

At any moment she felt the room might spin away into blackness. She could see everything Merta had seen at the river bank, still feel the cold of snow and smell the sweat of horses, still hear Tural's voice and see the dagger flashing down on Loen's back.

She could play it all through in her mind like a film in which everything seemed to happen at a normal speed but in which hours had become seconds.

Without knowing why, she felt she was being watched. She glanced around dreading to see Tural's face staring at her. The window was an accusing blank.

Laura pressed her hands between her knees to drive out her fear and saw again Loen's burning red hair and the way he'd looked at her when she called. She longed to return to him.

She put out her hand to touch the bracelet and then quickly drew it back. Suddenly she felt tired, cold with the horrible chill of wet, heavy clothes.

She undressed and rubbed herself dry, all the time trying to understand what had happened to her. For a time she'd become a girl called Merta who must have lived hundreds of years ago.

But where was the me who's Laura? She shook her head impatiently.

She put on dry clothes and then took a piece of string and made a loop through the bracelet. She put the loop over her head and dropped the bracelet down the neck of her shirt next to her skin. She looked at herself in the mirror to make certain the bracelet was safely hidden.

She was about to brush the tangles out of her hair when she heard James stamping down the corridor.

"Hurry up, Laura, you're late for breakfast."

He went back to the living room where they ate their meals.

And now I've got to eat breakfast with Julian, she thought as she opened her bedroom door.

"Have you hung up those wet clothes?" Julian snapped as Laura sat down.

Laura looked at James sitting opposite her. He was plastering cherry jam onto a long, narrow, crusty piece of French bread. She wished he'd cut his fringe so she could see his eyes. *If I could see his eyes I'd know if Julian's lost his temper with him too.*

"Not yet." Laura ignored Julian and looked around the table. "Aren't there any croissants today?"

Julian thrashed about in the paper he was reading, slapping it noisily when he turned it over.

"They forgot to bring any," James said with his mouth full.

Laura broke off a piece of baguette.

"I hear you fell in the river," her mother said vaguely as Laura split the piece of bread in half and started to butter it. Her mother never worried about what Laura or James did. They liked that. She trusted them.

Laura smiled quickly at her mother.

"I'm all right," she said, noticing how happy her mother looked.

"Julian and I are going to Annecy this morning; we thought you and James might want to come too."

"What for?" Laura asked doubtfully.

Her mother looked at Julian who bundled up his paper and threw it down on the floor.

"Don't you want to go to that fishing tackle shop,

Laura?" Her mother sounded surprised. "Just before you came in Julian was saying he thought you might need a new rod."

Laura saw James watching her expectantly.

"I want to stay here," she said. "I don't need a new rod."

Julian smiled foxily. "I'm meeting a man. He wants to buy some gold jewelry for a museum. Funnily enough I think I can get him exactly what he wants."

Laura glanced down, fearful that Julian had noticed the outline of the bracelet hidden under her shirt.

Her mind was a confusion of conflicting thoughts. *Does Julian know what I found?* she asked herself desperately. She still felt the pain of his shouting unjust accusations at her. *He's not going to bribe me to forget that by giving me a fishing rod.* She glanced defiantly at Julian. He was staring back at her in a cool, detached way.

"I'm staying here," Laura said stubbornly.

"James will have to stay with you, then. I can't leave you on your own." Julian spoke as if there could be no argument.

"Why?"

"Because I say so." Julian pushed back his chair.

Laura saw James pick up his cup and use it to hide his face as he drank.

"We'll be back at half-past twelve," Julian said, "and don't go near that river again."

"Do the washing up if you're not coming, won't you, Laura?" Her mother stood up and lightly kissed the top of Laura's head. "You gave poor Julian such a scare. He's terribly protective. Be good, both of you."

Laura and James sat opposite each other and listened to

their mother and Julian going upstairs, banging doors, getting ready to go out.

"Why didn't you want to go?" James said, pushing hair out of his eyes. "I wanted to."

Laura knew James liked wandering about the arcaded streets of Annecy while he gazed into shop windows selling things he'd never seen before.

"I'm sorry," she said absently. She was desperate to know if a knife had cut through Loen's cloak striking at ribs and lungs.

The bracelet was cold against her skin.

Laura was starting to wash up the breakfast dishes when she heard the car drive away. James had disappeared.

She looked at the sink glistening with bubbles. A coffee cup was floating on the water. She jabbed the washing brush into the cup which filled and sank, leaving oily brown suds. She gazed for a moment at the bubbles bursting stupidly, at the submerged shapes of cups and saucers and plates and the jumble of knives and spoons.

For a moment she stayed leaning over the sink hating steam and dishes and hot slippery water. Then she dropped the brush and ran out of the kitchen through the living room to her bedroom.

She sat down on the bed and pulled the loop of string over her head. The bracelet spun slowly around, first one way then the other. The battered face held between the ears of wheat scowled at her.

How did I become Merta? she asked herself. She stared at the face as if it could answer. There was a great cavern of doubt in her mind filled with shadowy questions she could not answer.

Gradually the bracelet came to rest and hung motionless before her. Impulsively she slipped it onto her left wrist. The gold was hard and heavy on her skin. She stood up and went to look at herself in the small mirror on top of the chest of drawers. As she held up her arm to see the bracelet a sudden shiver of gooseflesh flew from her finger tips to her shoulder.

She felt awkward and unnatural holding up her arm to see the bracelet in the small, inadequate mirror, so she pulled off the bracelet and laid it on top of the chest of drawers. It looked worn and harmless on the brown wood.

She gazed at the reflection of her face. *Did Loen see my face or someone else?* she asked herself. She tried to fix Loen clearly in her mind, to feel again the meaning in his eyes when he looked at her. For a moment she saw him clearly against snowy trees; then he vanished and she was looking at Tural's bloodless skin, the red, hate-clenched lips in the moment when he drove his dagger at Loen's back.

She shut her eyes and shook her head to drive away the memory of Tural's face. *But I must know,* she thought. She opened her eyes and looked distractedly at the top of the chest of drawers and noticed something quite trivial—her hairbrush.

She never left her hairbrush lying on its back with the bristles sticking in the air. She wasn't fussy but she hated looking into the bristle-skewered hairs. Now it was lying on its back. She was certain it was the other way up when she went to breakfast.

Impulsively she pulled open the two top drawers.

The left one was empty. In the right were two newish shirts and a pile of little boxes. She kept a coral necklace in one and a ring her father had given her in another. The box on top had come with her watch. It was lying on its side, open. The piece of rock crystal and the sliver of moss agate she kept in it were spilled out carelessly.

Her face in the mirror was deathly pale.

"Who did it?" she asked her relection. She saw faces in the mirror behind hers, her mother, Julian, a shadowy face, the mouth wrenched open in hate. The hair pricked on her neck.

The room seemed to contract and shut her in like a prison cell. Again Laura felt there were eyes spying on her, waiting to steal the bracelet lying on the chest of drawers.

Then it came to her.

He searched my room, she said to herself. Julian must have crept in here before he went to Annecy.

She snatched up the bracelet and looked around. James was standing in the doorway.

4 ‡ Hiding Place

"What's that?" James walked quickly toward her.

Laura said nothing. She stood not knowing what to do, wishing only that she could hide the bracelet from James.

"Can I see it?" James held out his hand.

Reluctantly she gave it to him.

"I found it in the river," she said, turning away and staring out of the window.

"Oh, Laura, you are lucky, it's gold! It must be!"

James flopped down on the bed. Laura watched him try the bracelet on both his wrists.

"It's beautiful," James said slowly. "I wonder when it was made."

He held the bracelet up to the light, quite unaware of how anxiously Laura was watching him.

Then he saw the face. He blinked in surprise and smiled happily at Laura.

"It's like Ghenghis Khan," James said, "he looks so angry you think blood will spurt out of his eyes at any moment." James was fond of that story. "Have you told Julian and Mother? They'll want to see it."

Laura couldn't restrain herself. She snatched the bracelet from James.

"They're not going to."

James looked at her in amazement.

"Why not?"

"You heard why he's gone to Annecy. He'd make me sell it. All he cares about is money."

"He wouldn't. You found it, it's yours, not his!"

"I'm not telling anyone I found it. I can't trust him. He wants to order me about all the time. He even searched my room this morning."

Laura turned away from James.

"What do you mean, searched your room?" James looked at his sister guardedly. He had never known her so suspicious and secretive.

Laura waved her arm wildly at the chest of drawers.

"He scrambled all the boxes in that drawer."

"Don't be a nit. You've got nothing he'd want. Besides he doesn't even know you found a gold bracelet."

"It could only be him. I tell you I'm not telling Julian I found this, or Mother!" Laura heard herself shout. "I can't trust her now."

Laura took a deep breath and searched for a way of convincing James. "You never told Aunt Lydia you had Prince Albert."

James smiled despite himself.

Their mother had gone abroad to work after their father died. James and Laura never understood why, she just seemed to want to escape, to be by herself. They were moved like bits of awkward furniture to their Aunt Lydia's. James felt sick whenever he thought about the curtains in Aunt Lydia's sitting room.

Their aunt's garden was all neat concrete paths and precisely clipped plants. One day James had found a toad gulping with disappointment because he could find no large squashy leaves to meditate under.

James called the toad Prince Albert and made a comfortable home for it in his bedroom. He never told his aunt. A day or two later when she was out shopping he thought Prince Albert might like a bath. He had just filled the washbasin in the bathroom and put Prince Albert on the ledge where the plug and soap were kept when Laura called him. He forgot all about Prince Albert.

Later, when Aunt Lydia went to wash some imaginary dirt off her face, she found the Prince dozing in her wash cloth. James always swore her screams cracked two windows in the house on the other side of the street.

"Albert was special," James said with a dreamy expression on his face. "I wonder what he's doing now."

"You must help me, James. Julian'll go all moral and make me give it to him one way or another."

James glanced quickly at Laura. She was so at a loss, so convinced that Julian was threatening her, that he found himself half believing what she told him.

"Why not hide it?"

"How?" Laura waved her hand around the room. It was so bare—bed, table, chair, chest of drawers. There were no good places to hide anything.

James pushed the hair out of his eyes and thought about the bed he was sitting on. It was like a ship's bunk built into the wall beneath the window which was divided into two casements which opened into the room. The head of the bed was made by the wooden wall separating Laura's room from his own.

He absentmindedly thumped the wall. It boomed like a drum.

"It's hollow," James said excitedly.

"How does that help?"

"I can cut a hole in the wall. You can hide the bracelet inside."

James dived under the bed.

"It'll be easy," he said as he pulled himself out and stood up. "I'll get some tools from the barn."

He didn't think much of Laura's quarrel with Julian, but he liked the idea of making a secret hiding place.

When he came back Laura was rolling up the rug.

"You must hurry," she said urgently, looking at her watch. "They'll be back soon. It's nearly half-past ten."

"We'll manage," James said, squirming under the bed. "Put the lamp on the floor, I can't see what I'm doing."

Laura listened to James drilling and sawing. She felt the minutes flying by. At any moment she expected Julian and her mother to return. James seemed to be destroying the whole house; the noise he made was deafening.

At last James came out from under the bed. Sawdust stuck to his eyelashes and he was picking sawdust off the tip of his tongue.

Laura squatted down.

"God almighty, James!"

He had cut a rectangular slot in the wall. It looked enormous and raw and obvious.

It was the sort of hole that would drive Julian into an even greater rage than Laura's falling into the river. This time Laura felt Julian might have a just cause.

"Can you really hide that?" she asked anxiously.

"Have you got a measure?" James said, as if it would be no trouble at all.

Laura gave him her very chipped and scarred school ruler.

He slid back under the bed to measure the hole.

"I'm going to the barn," he said as he came out. "I won't be long."

"Do hurry, James."

When he had gone, Laura noticed the floor. It was covered with a thick film of sawdust. She ran to the kitchen for the vacuum cleaner and sucked up the sawdust and the fluff which had escaped from under the bed. She also found three felt-tip pens she'd lost two weeks ago.

She sat down and fidgeted, waiting for James to come.

He's taking hours, she thought, looking at her watch for the hundredth time. *It's nearly a quarter to twelve and Julian said he'd be back at half-past.* She had just decided to run to the barn to hurry James when he strolled casually into the room as if he had all the time in the world. He was carrying an oblong box and two narrow pieces of wood.

"What's that?" Laura asked.

"It's a drawer to slide into the wall."

"Is it big enough?"

"Of course," James said scornfully. "Try it while I fix these runners."

Laura put the bracelet into the drawer. It was a perfect fit.

She was always amazed at the skill with which James could use tools. The sides of the drawer were sharp and accurately cut, and he had joined all the pieces together so that there were no screws showing on the outside.

"Give me the drawer," he called.

She bent down and gave it to him. She watched him slip it into the wall. Where there had been a gaping hole there was now a smooth board. Laura looked away and then back at the wall. She had to search to find the drawer.

"Can you see it?" James asked proudly.

"Only just, if I look hard. How do you pull it out?"

"Put your nails in at the side."

James showed her.

"Give me the bracelet, I'll put it in."

Reluctantly Laura let James put the bracelet into the drawer. She wished she was more certain it would be safe hidden in the wall. She looked at her watch. It was ten past twelve.

"They'll be here in a minute."

Laura frantically cleaned up the mess and put back the rug.

"God!" Laura said as she switched off the vacuum cleaner. "I've forgotten the washing up."

She ran into the kitchen. The water in the sink was cold. She turned on the hot tap and ran water over the plates, knives, cups, and saucers and handed them to James to dry.

He was doing the last saucer when they heard the car scrunching down the track to the barn.

"I forgot the tools," James said.

"Take them back now."

They met Julian and their mother walking down to the house. Their mother was carrying a basket filled with parcels wrapped in the special pink paper used by one of the Annecy butcher's shops. Laura thought they both looked rather pleased with themselves.

I'll never tell Julian what I found, she said to herself, *he'd sell it to the first man who asked for it.*

Julian stopped in the middle of the path and gazed pointedly at the tools James was carrying.

"What were you doing with those, James?"

Laura held her breath. She heard James say, "The catch was loose on Laura's bedroom window. I thought I'd fix it for you."

"You didn't need a saw for that surely."

James blushed.

"I thought I might, I didn't actually."

James started to walk past Julian.

"Be sure you put them back in the right place," Julian said over his shoulder. "Well, Laura, we had a very successful meeting." He rubbed his hands together.

Laura shut her eyes and walked after James.

Her mother called out happily, "I bought some absolutely super veal for supper."

"Incidentally," Laura's mother said, putting down her glass, "Madame Boulard telephoned. She wants you to go down for your French lesson tomorrow morning, not in the afternoon."

They were eating supper. Laura dimly heard what her mother said. She felt she was miles away from her family even though they were all sitting closely around a table. She didn't care about tomorrow's French lesson. Julian started telling a story about a visit he'd made to Tokyo. His voice seemed to be coming from a great distance.

Sitting at the table was like looking through a window into a brilliantly lit room. She watched Julian and James and her mother gesture, laugh, eat, but she kept herself aloof, let walls build themselves between her and the circle of talk which had Julian for its center.

She only wanted to yield to the longing which was drawing her away from the light deep into a darkness which would suddenly burst open on Merta's life, which seemed far more important to Laura than living with her family and hearing James laugh at Julian's jokes. Pointless jokes made by a man she distrusted, a man who never enjoyed ordinary simple things as her father had.

Suddenly she couldn't stand the chatter, the family eating together any longer. She dropped her knife on the table and ran out of the room.

5 ‡ Arne

Laura switched on the light beside her bed. When she was undressed she took the bracelet out of its hiding place and put the loop of string around her neck.

She hurried into the bathroom, washed herself skimpily and brushed her teeth. She threw the toothbrush down on the shelf above the basin, remembered she had not flushed the toilet, yanked the handle and went back to her room. As she shut the door behind her she touched the face on the bracelet.

Her room vanished. She was staring at a brilliant point of light surrounded by blackness. The light was growing bigger. A wind was gusting and screaming around corners. She felt the heat of flames on her face.

For a second she struggled to remember the whiteness of

the sheets on her bed, but a knife sliced through her memory cutting off Laura and she was Merta staring into the heart of a fire.

Gusts of freezing air made the flames swirl, casting dark shadows. She looked up and saw a face, sallow, with lank black hair touching sunken cheeks. Arne the goldsmith was crouching on the other side of the fire. They were alone in a low circular hut made of withies daubed with clay and it was night.

As if he had just been asked a question, Arne lifted his head and spoke.

"Well, the dagger never touched Loen when Tural tried to kill him by the river." Arne's voice was dimmed by the fury of the wind.

She shuddered remembering the cold gray blade flashing down, tearing through Loen's uplifted cloak. That was just after the first snows fell; now it was almost midwinter.

"I hate Tural," she said shortly. "He'll come here sometime. He said Loen must pay him."

She was sitting on a low stool and her legs were cramped. She didn't want to move away from the warmth of the blazing charcoal fire which burned without smoke. Intense white flames wrapped a crucible filled with gold which Arne was melting to pour into two squat molds warming beside the fire.

She could only think of what Arne had been telling her about Tural. Everyone else brushed her questions aside, even Loen. Tural was hidden from her by a wall of silence. Only Arne, occasionally, would tell her what little he knew.

"Did you ever see his mother?" she asked.

"Once, the day he caught me."

She listened to the strange way Arne spoke her language. He would never let her hear the sound of his own tongue. Every time she asked he refused. He wouldn't even tell her where he was born. He only said a long way to the east and his eyes would roam bitterly around the comfortless hut where he worked.

"Tell me about her."

"She's white like her son," he paused and then added, "and she's beautiful."

Arne shielded his eyes from the glare of the burning charcoal and delicately pushed a slender rod into the crucible glowing at the center of the flames.

His arms and hands were flecked with hundreds of tiny scars.

"It will be flowing soon," he said, laying down the rod on the earth floor.

She hardly heard him. She was still caught by Arne's description of Tural's mother who had come after Loen's mother died bringing her white son as a stepbrother for Loen.

She raised her head and looked at Arne fearfully.

"Did she ever say anything to you?"

"We talked together. She asked me what I could do."

She noticed an inward glint come to the smith's eyes.

"She must have poisoned Loen's father."

Arne turned his head away so his lank black hair fell over his face. He picked something off the ground behind him. He was holding three straws which he started twisting over and over each other to make a circle.

"And Loen revenged himself on both of them," Arne said slowly. "He drove them into the forest, let them take nothing."

"Who told you that?"

"People talk to me, even if they do find the way I speak strange." His voice was full of scorn. "Perhaps Loen was too kind. Some say he should have thrown them strangled and weighted into a pond."

A great gust of wind shook the hut making the flames leap and dart.

"I suppose you wish Tural and his mother were rotting beneath black water," Arne suggested in his strange voice, "his hair tangled in weed, her beauty swamped and bloated."

She hugged her arms around her knees. His words frightened her.

Arne put the circle of straw he had made on the ground.

"Stand back, Merta," he ordered.

She moved a few paces away as Arne took a pair of tongs and reached into the flames.

Very carefully he picked up the crucible. It shone white with heat. Arne's eyes were squinting against the glare, and lit by the shimmering of molten gold his face seemed immensely strong and purposeful.

His lips parted slightly and his tongue darted between his lips as he held the crucible above the smaller of the two molds.

The sinews in his arms tightened. His knuckles pressed taut the white scars on the back of his hands. She heard the wind rise to a high drawn scream as the crucible tilted till a thick golden crust gathered at its lip and hung there before a column of liquid gold fell into the head of the mold.

For a second he glanced up and looked straight into her eyes.

"Loen had to find a smith to make these for you," he said. His eyes flicked back to the blazing metal dropping into the mold. "Tural knew that, and his mother. She most of all. Then she knows so many things."

But she hardly heard what Arne said above the roaring storm. Her eyes burned with light from the gold. She watched Arne's hand slowly bending over as he tipped the crucible. A pool of shimmering gold formed on top of the mold. He stopped pouring, and she saw his chest fall in a long shuddering sigh as he moved the crucible till it was poised over the second and larger mold.

A column of brilliant light fell through the darkness. Suddenly Arne started whispering. His lips moved furtively, coaxingly. He seemed to be repeating the same words over and over again.

Her heart jumped as she understood. Arne was talking to the gold, urging it to do as he willed. Then the flowing column thinned, wavered for an instant and shrank to a glowing drop. Arne's lips were still.

He put the empty crucible on the earth floor and flexed his hand to ease the tense muscles in his arm.

Then he looked at her. She flinched as his eyes met hers. She felt she had never really seen him before. He was no longer a ragged, sallow-faced man from a far country who was only of interest to her because he had talked with Tural and had a craft. He seemed stronger even than Loen, able to bend people to his will as easily and certainly as he worked gold. She shrank from him.

Arne turned his head away and stared at the doorway. Above the demented wind she heard footsteps coming toward the hut.

Arne smiled to himself and hobbled awkwardly to the

door. She heard him slide back a latch and then a blast of air, cold as green ice, swept into the hut. Loen stood in the doorway. Flakes of snow flew past him to die hissing in the fire. He was wearing a heavy cloak of skins and he was unarmed.

Immediately she felt safe, protected by him. All the terror which clenched her mind while she thought of Tural and his mother vanished. Loen stood close to her and looked at the molds cooling from white to sullen red. He put his arm around her shoulders. She felt his hand's weight, the tips of his fingers resting on her collar bone, the warmth of his hand flowing into her.

Loen said, "Show Merta what you have made, Arne."

She glanced at his face and then at Arne.

Arne was holding the circle of straws. The wind died. Arne was speaking a language she had never heard before. The strange words hung in the air. Then he dropped the straws. For a moment they made a golden circle on the molds, then they writhed, shrivelled in the heat and a circle of flame ran around them and they were a circle of ashes lying on the blackening molds.

Arne leaned forward and blew the ash away. Again the storm broke around the hut.

"Why did you do that?" She was shouting. "Why did you do that?"

Arne glanced up with the startled look of someone who gives a present only to see it thrown away.

"It would mean nothing to you," he said scathingly.

"But what did you say?"

"That!" he laughed. "You wanted to hear the language my people speak."

She clutched Loen's arm.

"He spoke to Tural's mother before he came here," she said accusingly.

Loen looked sharply at Arne and then put his hand on hers.

"How can she harm us. She's far away."

"I wish she was dead." Her voice rose high above the wind.

Arne's head jerked up.

"She can never harm us, Merta." Loen's hand was moving over hers.

She knew he was trying to calm her. She pressed her cheek against Loen's arm hoping he was right.

"Arne, show her what you have made," Loen insisted.

Arne put his hand close to the molds to feel how hot they were.

Slowly, grudgingly, he broke them open. There was the cast gold holding its taut shape. A heavy bracelet and a great golden collar lying in the dust and cinders around the furnace.

They were rich and beautiful and Loen had ordered Arne to make them for her. She wanted to slide the bracelet over her wrist and clasp the collar around her neck. They would bind her and Loen together. She longed for the moment when she would wear them for the first time.

Impulsively Loen reached down to pick up the bracelet, but Arne's hand flashed out like a talon gripping Loen's wrist.

"Leave it!" he shouted. His words burst out like a bitter froth burning them with its intensity. The wind howled and the flames leapt in blue points.

Arne took a piece of soft leather and using it to protect his hand lifted up the bracelet. He turned it sideways and

she saw it was made of three ears of plaited wheat and in
their center a face with bulging eyes and high cheekbones
and hair swept back from the forehead. The shining gold
was like the innocent surface of a lake, smooth reflecting
light hiding something mysterious. Amongst the grains of
golden wheat were the dancing points of flames.

Arne put down the bracelet and held up the collar. It
was wide and subtly curved to lie around her neck, and it
bore the same cunningly plaited straws and ears of wheat
surrounding the same savage golden face.

As she looked at the golden eyes and sweeping hair she
heard the drumming of hoofs beating far away. The wind
tossed the sound this way and that.

They all heard them. Loen's face hardened. Arne
glanced anxiously over his shoulder.

She listened to the horses surging through the forest. A
troop of riders was galloping between the black frozen
trees. For a moment she thought they were riding toward
them, but the sound was constant, neither getting louder
nor softer.

"They're circling us," Loen said quietly.

She felt his arm pulling her hand as he turned to listen
to the hoofs beating the stone-hard ground. She was surrounded by a river of hoofbeats and screaming icy wind.
Cutting through the sound she heard a voice singing,
high-pitched and sweet. The voice chilled her to the bone.
It was like Tural's voice but even more piercing in its in-
sidious sweetness. The song was a needle driven into her
brain.

She put her hands to her ears but she was still torn by
the song weaving through the chaos of the storm.

Suddenly the wind slackened and the sound of the

horses faded away till they could hear only the ripple of flames above the fire.

Arne looked up at her.

"Tural has ridden out of the forest and he has brought his mother with him." Arne sounded afraid. "That was her voice, that was Flear's song."

The hut trembled and dissolved into blackness. For a moment she was struggling against the threat held in that name. Tural and his mother were poised to strike at her and Loen.

"Flear!"

Laura whispered the name. The bracelet hung from a piece of string around her neck. The golden ears of wheat held dull reflections of the electric light beside her bed.

6 ‡ *Madame Boulard*

Next morning when she woke up Laura snatched the string from her neck and looked intently at the bracelet. Even though they were now scratched and blunted she recognized the plaited stalks and the face held by the ears of wheat.

There could be no doubt. She was holding the bracelet Arne had made for Merta, but where was the golden collar?

Suddenly she was pierced by the sound of Flear's song. For an instant her room held the cold of a freezing winter storm. She cowered on the bed. The air thickened with the invisible presence of Flear and Tural. They were haunting her, threatening her as they threatened Merta and Loen. She could feel Tural's cold eyes staring at her. The walls blurred. She dreaded the sound of horses swirling around the house.

"I'm not Merta," she shouted, holding her head.

Flear's song snapped like a breaking wire. Laura was sweating with fear. Outside, the sun shimmered on the leaves of the walnut trees.

She remembered the warmth of Loen's hand.

She slid off the bed and hid the bracelet in the wall. She slowly dressed and brushed her hair. In the mirror her eyes were dark and fearful. She felt cut off from anyone who could tell her what she should do. James would be kind, ask sensible questions, but he could not guard her from the terror which had filled her room.

She thought of the day stretching before her, meals, chores, conversations. Then she remembered.

Madame Boulard.

She and James were going to Madame Boulard's for a French lesson at ten. Laura's heart lifted.

At half-past nine she was hurrying up the track from the house. When she came to the road she stopped.

"Come on, James," she shouted, "we'll be late."

She saw James, who was hanging about by the barn, turn and break into a run. Laura walked with long, quick strides down into the valley.

The road ran along the side of the mountain which flowed up in a great waving meadow of pale grass to a line of ochre cliffs burning in the sun.

Far below her Laura could see Madame Boulard's house at the edge of the village. It was painted white and stood next to a tall, ugly house with dark brown walls and a complicated slate roof. This house had been turned into a café and was owned by a man called Matthieu. Laura and

James sometimes bought drinks from him after their lessons with Madame Boulard. He was a morose, misanthropic man always writing figures on scraps of paper and obsessively doing sums.

When they reached Madame Boulard's, Laura pushed open the iron gate, which squeaked, and walked up the gravel path to the front door. As she pressed the bell, she breathed in the hot, peppery smell of the tall privet hedge surrounding the garden.

Laura heard Madame Boulard's light footsteps in the hall and then the door opened.

"Good morning, Laura, James," Madame Boulard said in French. "I hope it wasn't inconvenient for you coming this morning and not this afternoon."

Hearing Madame Boulard's clear, liquid voice Laura felt safer. The echoes of Flear's song died. She looked up at Madame Boulard and thought how much kinder a person she was than Julian. She had short blonde hair just turning gray and a face which always reminded Laura of a very intelligent, friendly bird.

Over the last few weeks Madame Boulard had overcome all Laura and James's diffidence and nerves at speaking a foreign language. Now she had them chattering away without pauses and stutterings as they labored to assemble strange combinations of shapes in their mouths.

They walked into the house which smelt of polish and delicious wafts of what Madame Boulard was cooking for her lunch.

"You start today, Laura," Madame Boulard said as they sat around a low table in the sitting room. "Tell me what you did yesterday."

"I went fishing before breakfast," Laura said. For a moment she wanted the whole story to tumble out, then she hesitated.

"Where?" Madame Boulard prompted.

"In the big pool by the fall."

"She fell in," James said. "Julian was furious."

"You mustn't worry about that," Madame Boulard said. "People sometimes make a great fuss about nothing. Did you catch a fish?"

The lessons always went like this. Laura and James told Madame Boulard what they had done and she asked questions, leading them on and on to more complicated constructions.

"Yes, but it got away, the line broke."

Laura stopped. She had to decide now. Madame Boulard's gray eyes were expectant, waiting. Her head was cocked on one side. She seemed to be interested in nothing but Laura and what had happened to her.

Before she could reflect, Laura said, "But I found something else." Then instantly she regretted it.

"How very exciting. What was it?" Madame Boulard leaned forward to encourage Laura.

Again Laura had to make a decision. She was sure the bracelet was being used by Tural and Flear. She remembered the horrors lurking in her room.

"I found an old bracelet," she said.

"That's better than a fish, but why aren't you wearing it now?"

"I can't."

"Is it rusty?"

"Oh, no."

"Well then . . ." Madame Boulard glanced at James as if she was asking him to explain.

Laura said quickly, "I've had to hide it."

"Is it so very valuable?"

"From Julian."

"Julian!"

"He might sell it. He knows people who want to buy old jewelry."

"Surely he wouldn't sell your bracelet," Madame Boulard said incredulously, "not anything of yours, Laura."

"I can't trust him," Laura said decisively.

Madame Boulard leaned back in her chair and looked thoughtfully at Laura.

"I think you're wrong about Julian, I've known him for a long time," she said slowly. "However, you've hidden it safely?"

"James made a hiding place for it in the wall of my bedroom."

"Well, you must be careful, there are all sorts of ways of finding things you know."

She turned to James. It would be his turn now.

"Nobody could find it," James said. "Could they, Laura?"

Laura shook her head. She wanted to rush out of the room and fly back to the house to make certain the bracelet was still safe.

"I'm sure you're right, James," Madame Boulard said. "But really hiding something is very difficult. For instance practically anyone can find water which is hidden under the ground."

"How?" James said dubiously.

"I'll show you."

Madame Boulard went to a desk in the corner of the

room. She came back holding a piece of copper wire about a meter long.

"What do you need that for?" James asked.

"You'll find out when we go into the garden. Come on, Laura, it's too hot indoors."

Laura watched James hurry after Madame Boulard. At the door Madame Boulard turned around.

"Come, Laura," she insisted. "Your bracelet's quite safe if you've only Julian to worry about."

Laura followed them to the lawn at the side of the house. Part of it was overshadowed by the drab brown walls of Matthieu's café. She sat on a seat under a honeysuckle arbor and watched James and Madame Boulard.

She heard Madame Boulard say, "This is what you do first, James."

Madame Boulard took the two ends of the copper wire and crossed them over each other so that the wire was shaped like the letter "V." She made James hold the ends of the wire in the palms of his upturned hands with the point of the "V" sticking out in front of him.

"There's a spring under this lawn, James," Madame Boulard said. "Walk slowly toward Laura and see if the wire moves."

Laura could see how James was trying to concentrate. His eyes squinted in the sunlight and his lips were pressed together. He held the wire so tightly his arms were trembling.

The wire didn't even twitch, and when he reached Laura James collapsed with disappointment.

"Never mind, James," Madame Boulard said kindly. "We'll try another way."

Laura wondered why Madame Boulard was holding James's hands so her thumbs pressed on the inside of his wrists at the place where the veins cross the tendons. Then she started walking backwards across the lawn drawing James after her. He grinned sheepishly at Laura. She knew he must feel a perfect ass.

All at once as James took a slow pace forward to keep up with Madame Boulard the wire shuddered. It twisted and struggled. She saw the muscles bunching in his forearms as he tried to stop the wire pointing at the grass. He couldn't resist the force pulling the wire down.

Madame Boulard let go of his hands.

"I knew you could do that, James," she said quietly. "Now try by yourself."

Madame Boulard came and sat beside Laura.

"Almost all of us can find water that way," she said as James walked toward them with the wire pointing out in front of him. "Other things take a bit more—what should I say—a bit more concentration."

Laura found it difficult to believe what Madame Boulard told her. James was far too matter-of-fact a person, she thought, to be able to find water in the mysterious way Madame Boulard had taught him. She didn't expect he could do it again without help. Yet over exactly the same spot the wire bent and pointed quivering at the ground. The power moving the wire was like the strength in a great gust of wind, invisible but able to send an oak tree sprawling on its side.

"I can do it!" he shouted. "It's easy!"

"Of course you can, James, do it a few more times."

As James walked across the lawn Laura and Madame Boulard heard a rustling noise in the privet hedge separating the garden from Matthieu's café. They looked around.

A large ginger cat stalked out from the hedge, sat down on the edge of the lawn and blinked its eyes patronizingly at Laura and Madame Boulard. It was one of those fluffy ginger cats, the kind with a tail like a flue brush and a very smug face.

"Oh, that cat," Madame Boulard said in an exasperated voice. "It keeps coming into my garden."

Laura recognized it as Matthieu's cat. Usually it lay on a window sill in the café, spurning all advances, rolling over, yawning, and generally looking conceited.

"Monsieur Matthieu!" Madame Boulard stood up and shouted angrily at the hedge. "Monsieur Matthieu, your cat's here again!"

Laura heard the crashing tinkle of a crate of empty bottles being dropped on the ground.

"Monsieur Matthieu!"

They heard Matthieu walking toward the hedge.

"Well, Madame Boulard, what do you want now?"

"Your cat. Yesterday she scratched up all my cyclamen."

"Don't you want to play with her?" Matthieu asked tauntingly.

"Of course not. She does far too much damage. The day before that I found her asleep on my lilies."

"Perhaps she wants to play with you."

"Don't be so clever, Monsieur Matthieu."

"You're lucky your garden's so pretty." There was a bitter edge to Matthieu's voice.

"I don't want it to happen again."

"Might as well try and stop the moon," Matthieu said. "I'm not wasting my time."

They heard him walking back to the café.

Madame Boulard shook her head resignedly. She turned to Laura. "Could you persuade it to go back to Matthieu?"

Laura scratched the cat's ears and smoothed its magnificent ginger tail. Then she picked it up, turned it around and pushed it back through the hedge. It meowed pitifully but squirmed through without losing any of its dignity.

"Thank you so much, Laura." Madame Boulard paused and turned so she was facing her. "Tell me, why do you think Julian wants to sell your bracelet?"

"I'm frightened," Laura said unexpectedly.

"But why? How can you be frightened of Julian?"

"It's not only Julian. There's something about the bracelet I can't understand."

"Tell me, Laura."

"I don't know," Laura paused. She looked into Madame Boulard's kind, intelligent eyes. "You promise you'll not tell anyone else."

Madame Boulard nodded.

Then Laura said hesitantly, "I think it makes me become someone else—a girl who lived a long time ago." She stopped not knowing how to go on.

"Yes?" Madame Boulard said expectantly.

"This girl, she's called Merta, has enemies. This morning I felt they were threatening me too." Laura found it all so difficult to explain. She didn't want Madame Boulard to laugh at her as James might if she told him.

"You can't really mean that, Laura," Madame Boulard said. "What makes you feel threatened?"

"I feel eyes watching me."

"But you don't see anyone."

"No, but I'm sure someone's there."

"When you think you are this girl Merta, can you see and hear and feel as clearly as you can now?"

"There's no difference."

"You're sure you're not imagining things. We sometimes do—we all do."

Laura shook her head. She wanted to contradict Madame Boulard but before she could speak Madame Boulard said, "Now, about Merta. You say the bracelet grants you visions of another time and place. A lot of people have that sort of experience, though I don't think it could make you become someone else. It must be a very unusual bracelet if it can. I wish you had brought it with you."

"It is an unusual bracelet," Laura said bluntly.

"I understand, Laura, I believe you, and I hate to think of your being frightened."

Suddenly Laura felt almost happy for the first time that day. She was glad she had confided in Madame Boulard.

"I knew you'd be the only one I could talk to about it," she said.

Their eyes met in trust.

"Why are you so suspicious of Julian?"

"Yesterday, I found my room had been searched. Mother or James wouldn't do that."

"You mustn't become suspicious, Laura. You must be discreet." She looked intently at Laura.

"There are so many ways," Laura paused, "Julian could find things. Even you said so."

"Oh, Laura!" James said, coming up unexpectedly. "You act as if Julian's got a metal detector."

"I never said that," Laura said sharply.

"What could he do then?" James asked. "Magic it out of the wall?"

"He could do what you did just now, James." Madame Boulard said gravely.

James held up the wire.

"I was finding water. The bracelet's metal."

Madame Boulard seemed to forget James. "This girl Merta," she said. "All that could be dangerous, Laura. You must show me the bracelet, then I might be able to discover more about what's been happening to you." She looked up at James. "Some people can find metal—as easily as you found water."

There was a rustling in the privet hedge behind them. Madame Boulard jumped to her feet.

The rustling stopped. They heard Matthieu calling his cat.

Madame Boulard turned back to James.

"How?" he insisted.

"It's not difficult, James. You simply hold a pendulum."

7 ‡ *The Harp*

There was a waning moon that night. Laura lay in bed with her head propped up on the pillows. The moonlight fell across her in a narrow band. She could see the meadows, the crest of the mountain on the other side of the valley, and the line of trees marking the river. Everything was motionless except for the river which made the only sound. Laura sat up to see more of this remote, brittle moonlit world. The grass was shining with dew and the leaves on the walnut trees hung still as midnight. Far away, breaking the lilting rush of the river, a dog barked.

I must see the bracelet in moonlight, she thought. She got out of bed and put her nails to the edges of James's secret drawer. It slid open without making a sound. She held her breath and slowly inched her fingers into the drawer till they touched and seized the hard golden circle lying there.

The bracelet was colorless in the moonlight. The gold looked as ordinary as aluminum. But the shape was still strong however pale the light shining on it; even its shadow was powerful. Laura twisted the bracelet around to watch the shadow on the floor beside her bed. She made it tighten from a circle to an ellipse as taut as two drawn bows.

As the gold became warm in Laura's hands she remembered the sound of Flear's song swirling around the goldsmith's hut. Laura rubbed her thumb over the face on the bracelet. Beyond the window the moon turned the sky into a silver gauze. The moonlight made great black pools of shadow under the walnut trees. The mountains were sharp as a dragon's back, mossy and old with forests. She had the bracelet but the collar was still lost. At any moment the room might ring with the sound of Flear's song and her blood freeze under searching eyes. Laura ached with longing to be with Loen, safe.

A thin cloud like a flake of shell moved slowly toward the moon. Laura pushed up the sleeve of her nightdress and thrust her hand through the bracelet, sliding it over her arm till it was just below her elbow. The edge of the cloud touched the moon and sailed across its face to shine milky white edged with a pale violet halo.

The moon and cloud vanished. Laura couldn't move. She was in absolute blackness. She tried to call James. She tried to stare through the blackness. She tried to feel the bed, the window sill pressing against her shoulder. There was nothing.

Suddenly she was slipping. Her mind was being pushed

aside like a weight sliding across ice. For a moment she struggled instinctively to remain herself, to hold on to everything which made her Laura. Then her will snapped.

"It's your turn, Merta." Loen was handing her a dice box made of horn.

As she reached out to take it she saw the golden bracelet on her arm. She was still unused to wearing it. The ears of wheat held the hard polish of newly made gold and the little face Arne had placed between the plaited ears looked fierce and angry. The golden collar was clasped around her neck. She could feel it rising and falling slightly as she breathed.

She shook the dice box and watched the bracelet glitter in the flickering light of the torches burning in sconces on the walls.

The dice rattled and she quickly flicked the box down on the table.

"Four," Loen said.

They were playing trout and otter with ivory counters which they moved up and down a board.

She wondered which of her trout to move, then took the leader and pushed it along the board through four pools.

"Do you think he'll come soon?" she asked as she gave the dice box back to Loen.

"It doesn't matter when Tural comes," Loen said, picking up the box. "I've driven him out once, I can drive him out again."

While he shook the dice her eyes wandered around Loen's hall. The walls were strongly made of tree trunks set on end; the door was heavy and barred. There was light from torches and warmth from a fire of blazing logs. Yet ever since she had heard Flear's song coming through the storm she had been afraid. Always, even when Loen had clasped the collar around her neck and slipped the bracelet on her arm. She remembered the scourging sweetness of Flear's voice, the threatening face of Tural at the river. She felt she and Loen were walking along a thin blade of ice, never knowing when it would break.

She glanced up at the roof supported on great beams. A thin eddy of smoke from the fire curled up through a hole where she could see one brilliant winter star.

Some of Loen's men were sitting around the fire. One was making a bow string. Sethor carefully sharpened a spear. She could hear their voices through the rattling of the dice inside the box. *Perhaps I'm safe,* she thought, *perhaps nothing will happen.*

"Five." Loen moved the otter up the board. "I've caught one of your trout."

She shook her head at him, and smiled. He had uncanny luck with games.

As she picked up the dice box there was a clear knock, knock, knock. Immediately everyone was quiet.

"It's Tural!" Her eyes were wide and fearful.

Loen made a sign to Sethor. She held her breath and watched him walk, still holding the spear, toward the door.

The knocking came again.

"Only someone wanting shelter," Loen said casually. "Tural won't knock when he comes."

She heard the hinge grating as the door was slowly, cautiously opened.

An old woman so wrapped up in a cloak that they could not see her face shuffled into the hall. She was shivering with cold.

"Let her sit by the fire and give her something to eat and drink," Loen said. He turned back to Merta. "Throw the dice."

But she had forgotten the game. She was too relieved to find it was only an old woman who came to them from the cold and snow of a winter's night to beg food and shelter. She watched the old woman hobble across to the fire and sit with her face turned away from the wide oak table where she and Loen were sitting.

The old woman stretched long white fingers out to the flames. She rubbed her hands together and kneaded her fingers, squeezing out the cold. Then she reached under her cloak and pulled out a small harp.

"She must play to us, Loen," Merta said happily. "Ask her to play, I don't want to finish the game."

She touched the hair on the back of Loen's wrist. It was like fine red gold wire, each hair more uniquely and beautifully reflexed than the next.

"Of course, Merta." Loen dropped the dice into the box. "Play your harp for us, Granny." His voice was commanding.

The old woman bent down stiffly and picked up the harp. The wooden frame was dark from use.

Loen put his hand on the narrow curve of Merta's thigh. They sat close together on the bench while the old woman held the harp close to her ear and quietly tuned the strings. Then without telling them what she was going to play, her long fingers hooked across the harp and a soft chord drifted through the hall.

The men sitting on the benches by the fire stopped talking and turned to listen to the old woman muffled up in her cloak. Merta leaned her elbows on the table and cupped her chin in her hands. She felt the bracelet slide down her arm.

Again the old woman's long white fingers moved across the strings. Notes floated over them, the strings died and the notes faded into silence. They were all sitting so still that a log breaking into sparks and ashes sounded like a thunderclap.

Merta saw the old woman dart her head angrily at the fire as if she wanted to scold it for breaking the intense silence she had made.

The strings were plucked a third time and the sound was so clear and pure Merta wanted it to go on forever, to stay listening to the broken chord moving through the stillness of the torchlit hall, and never to move from the bench where she sat with Loen. If she could stay within the sound, she would never dread Loen's journeys into the forest again, never feel the debt he owed Tural looming over her like a great cloud charged with storm and fire.

She opened her lips to implore the old woman to play the chord again, but before she could speak a quick flurry of notes flew toward her. She glanced happily at Loen to see if he shared her delight at the dancing tune the old woman played.

Merta watched the old woman's hands moving quickly over the strings. Her shoulders were hunched around the harp to make it part of herself.

The notes weaved around them tying them into a net of sound which held everyone in the hall, cutting them off from the cold winter and the snowy trees and frosty ground without. For a moment Merta wondered if Arne heard the music where he sat sullenly beside the fire in his hut on the other side of the yard outside the hall.

Gradually the tune changed, became less airy, less full of light and sun. The notes were longer, deeper; the net of sound was closing around them. She could not take her eyes from the old woman's hunched back or the movement of her fingers circling ever more slowly across the strings. The old woman was crooning to herself. Merta could just hear the voice above the music of the harp. She felt herself growing drowsy. The gold collar around her neck felt heavier. The bracelet on her arm weighed against her skin. She tried to move her hand to take the collar from her neck and strip the bracelet from her arm. But she felt too tired, too drawn into the spell the music was weaving around her.

The music was growing louder, the voice of the old woman more distinct. Merta tried to look at Loen once more, but the effort of turning her head was too much for her. She could no longer feel his presence beside her. The music had separated her from Loen, wrapping her within itself.

The old woman's crooning changed to a wordless song, grew more distinct, the voice stronger. The hunched figure in the shabby threadbare cloak grew in strength, became less the body of an old woman who had begged for food and a night's lodging.

The music quickened, the song grew louder still, dragging Merta away from Loen.

She tried to pull herself back, to resist the music binding her to itself. She struggled to break the net drawing around her tighter and tighter. She wanted to shout, to bang her fists on the table, do anything to cut through the web of sound.

Then the song changed again, it grew softer, gentler,

lulling her to sleep. She was slipping farther and farther from Loen as the music closed around her. But now she didn't want to resist, just let the sound sweep her into itself till she was lost within the notes flowing softly from the harp strings and the song.

Then the song broke. The strings of the harp trembled, hovered for a moment and the old woman's voice was slithering its way into her ears. She was transfixed by the song which hurt it was so sharply, piercingly sweet. She wanted to jam her fingers into her ears and stop the sound tearing her eardrums. But her leaden arms could not move. The bracelet and the collar weighed her down. She was bound by the music of the harpstrings, torn by the hideous sweetness of the song.

Suddenly she remembered dancing flames and the sound of wind howling around Arne's hut. She knew the voice. She had heard it when Arne made the bracelet and the collar. Flear was singing in Loen's hall.

She couldn't move, she couldn't run away, she couldn't touch Loen. She was caught by the music and the song. They had cut her off from Loen.

There was a sudden movement.

"Stop!" Loen's voice tore through the net of sound.

The old woman by the fire spun around. There was the cold, beautiful face, the lips just parted in a smile.

"Tural!" she shouted, her voice high and sharp. "Loen has paid you, Tural. Come and see them now, Tural."

The door into the hall burst open. Tural stood there. Behind him dull against the sky of a winter's night black and pricking with stars stood eight men and each one held a drawn sword.

Tural moved swiftly toward the fire, his cloak swirling and writhing. He walked with the deliberate cruelty of a cat stalking a bird.

He stood beside his mother.

"Loen's paid you, Tural," Flear's voice cut through the watchful stillness in the hall. "You're cursed, Merta. Try taking the bracelet from your arm and the collar from your neck."

Merta snatched at the bracelet to pull it from her arm. A searing pain bored through muscles and bone. The bracelet wouldn't move, it was welded to her skin. Her fingers tore frantically at the collar around her neck. It was a fetter throttling her.

"She'll die slowly." Tural's voice was sickly sweet. "She'll wane with the moon and then be in darkness."

Merta looked helplessly at Loen. His face was utterly calm as if Flear and Tural were not standing a few paces from him. He held out his hand to her and his fingers locked in hers.

He led her slowly, cautiously from behind the table as if he was giving her to Tural and Flear.

Tural's lips parted expectantly. Loen was edging Merta toward the wall, keeping himself between her and Tural. She let herself be drawn by Loen. The bracelet and the collar were leaden weights dragging her down. She was weak with fear. Tural and his mother were watching her. She felt their eyes moving over her face. Their eyes were like sea creatures torn from their shells, the pupils soft and fleshy.

Loen was whispering to her, "Stay by the wall, Merta, stay between the posts."

They were level with two of the posts holding up the roof. Suddenly Loen threw her into the gap between them and hurled himself at Tural.

She heard a bellow of rage from Tural's men standing in the doorway. Their cloaks curled like waves as they rushed forward. A bench crashed over. Tural's sword swung back in a cold arc of dark iron and screeched against Loen's sword. Flear screamed like a hunter urging hounds to a kill.

Sethor brushed past Merta. Someone was sobbing near the fire. She saw fingers clutching a neck and blood pouring down the arm. The torches flared as a gust of wind burst through the open door. She saw a spear darting down and a face with the mouth open, the tongue pushed forward. The butt of the spear jerked and the face glazed over.

She pressed her forehead against the wood to drive out what she had seen. But she could not shut out the sound of men fighting.

A cloaked face, white and bloodless, was creeping toward her. She heard the jangle of harp strings. A hand reached around the post. Fingers touched her clothes.

"Loen! Loen!" She screamed and swung her arm back and down. The bracelet cracked the white fingers. Flear's harp fell to the floor.

Like a pool of quicksilver the mass of men fighting each other split apart and broke into separate drops. Tural was plucking his mother to the door. Only four of his men followed him. Their cloaks were cut and ragged. One man's arm flapped at his side. They were beaten.

Tural and Flear threw themselves onto their horses and wheeled into the night. Tural's remaining men galloped behind him. One other rider came last. She knew the sallow face and dark hair. It was Arne.

She leaned back against the post and saw the broken harp lying on the floor. The blackened wood was splintered and the strings curled slackly. Her arm still burned, the collar clung to her neck.

Loen was coming toward her, stepping over the bodies of four men. His youthful face was filled with misery. He held her tightly to him.

She was freezing cold and watching a cloud slip across the moon.

Laura heard James moving about on the other side of the wall. The bracelet was lying heavy on her wrist.

8 ‡ *The Path*

They were in the village.

"Go and help your mother do the shopping," Julian had told them. "I've work to do in a hurry and I want this house absolutely quiet while I do it."

James waited in the burning hot street while his mother and Laura bought cheese. He looked into the shop window filled with white goat cheeses, goat cheeses with crusty, gray rinds, fat orange colored cheeses made from cow's milk, and the huge round cheeses called Comte, wide and thick as wheels, cut open to show a soft, primrose inside flecked with tiny holes.

Gazing into the window, James couldn't forget two things Madame Boulard had said the day before: "This girl Merta, all that could be dangerous," and "You simply hold a pendulum." He wondered who on earth Merta was.

I'll ask Laura the first chance I get, he told himself, as his mother came out of the shop and filled his arms with parcels.

As for the pendulum, James resigned himself to waiting for his next lesson with Madame Boulard, when for once he'd be only too happy to start asking the questions.

They walked up the street to buy fruit. Outside the shop, trays on trestles held baskets of raspberries, currants, and velvety blue berries called *myrtilles.* James chose some wild strawberries and then helped his mother with the intricate business of finding a perfectly ripe melon, sniffing them, pressing them gently with a finger tip as if they were the heads of newborn babies.

The shop James liked best was at the end of the street, near Matthieu's café. It sold cow's horns and machines for making shotgun cartridges, hunting knives with deer's-foot handles and wineskins called *gourdes.* These were covered with hair and had mouthpieces of real horn. They hung from loops of gaily colored cord like bunches of furry fruit. James had always wanted one.

He stood outside the shop and shifted all the parcels into the crook of his arm so he could reach into his pocket. He had just enough to buy one of the middlesized *gourdes.* Laura and his mother were next door buying magazines.

He hurried into the shop. An old lady dressed in dusty black hovered beside him while he decided which one to buy.

"That's good," she said as she unhooked the gourd James had chosen. "You're a wise boy to buy that one."

Her knuckles were swollen with rheumatism; it was difficult for her to count the confusion of small change James poured onto the counter. James slung the wineskin on his shoulder and stroked the fur which smelt of animal.

"What on earth did you buy that for?" Laura asked rather enviously when she saw him.

"Because I wanted it, of course."

"I hope it didn't cost too much," his mother said vaguely.

James shook his head. He had learned long ago to buy things without telling anyone. If he did tell there always seemed to be a million good reasons why he shouldn't spend his money.

"Let's have a drink at Matthieu's," his mother said. "I'm parched."

They walked up the road to the café and sat down outside, under the shade of a lime tree, at a round metal table which had once been painted brown. There was a hole in the middle for an umbrella, but Matthieu had long since given up umbrellas to shade his customers. The tree was enough.

Matthieu ambled out from the café and took their orders. He was tall and gaunt and as usual took no apparent interest in his customers. Laura stretched her long legs under the table and wondered why Matthieu always wore brown. Every time she'd seen him he was wearing a brown shirt, brown trousers, brown socks and brown plastic sandals moulded to look like stitched leather.

Matthieu came back carrying a tray. He gave James his lemonade.

"So, you've bought a *gourde*," Matthieu said as he poured a Coke for Laura and a beer for their mother.

Matthieu counted out change on the table and then sat

in the café doorway and started copying figures from a newspaper.

James was sure he and Laura and their mother were the only people who ever bought anything from Matthieu. Their mother always said she liked his café because it was so authentic, but James found it rather sad.

Laura asked, "What did Julian mean when he said he had work to do?"

"It's this man whose museum wants to buy gold rings or bracelets or something."

Laura stiffened.

"Julian's heard about an interesting piece someone wishes to sell."

"Why did the museum especially ask Julian?" Laura picked up her glass as casually as she could. Her heart felt as if it was about to bound out of her chest.

"Because Julian's a kind of Father Christmas."

"Father Christmas!" Laura exclaimed, jerking her head up and making a horrible gurgling noise with her drinking straw.

"Well, he is. Mr. So-and-So living in Kansas City, or Edinburgh, or Antwerp, wants a piece of Roman glass, say, for his collection. With any luck he'll ask Julian to find it for him. That's how he earns his living—and yours."

"Who told Julian about the jewelry?" Laura asked.

"He doesn't want anyone except me to know till it's all settled."

"Well he's not . . ." Laura began and stopped. She was pale and tense.

Her mother looked sharply at her. "What's the matter

with you, Laura? You've really been rather trying lately, rushing out of rooms, not finishing your supper, skulking. Haven't you forgiven Julian yet for what he said the other morning? It's not like you to be so grudging." She finished her beer and stood up. "What a nuisance, I've forgotten to buy any cigarettes. I'll have to go back into the village. Wait here both of you."

James waited till his mother was out of earshot.

"Who's Merta?" He was making interlocking circles on the tabletop with his empty glass.

Laura shivered. Madame Boulard had told her to be discreet, and she was sure Madame Boulard was right.

"Nobody special," she said.

"How do you know her? Why haven't I met her?"

Laura clenched her fists under the table and prepared herself to silence James, even though it meant hurting him. If he knew about Merta or her fear of Tural coming from Merta's world into hers he'd think she was sickening for something and probably tell their mother and Julian. Julian would like that, he'd get the bracelet and sell it to this museum.

"Well, where did you meet her?" James said, sweeping the glass across the table, smearing the carefully made circles. "What's the mystery?"

"You're almost as prying as Aunt Lydia. And so boring."

James flushed angrily.

"What about the boring noise you made last night?"

"Oh, shut up, James." Laura swung around in her chair so she didn't have to look directly at him.

"Did you leave the bracelet in the wall?"

"Mmm."

"I think it's giving you nightmares, you kept me up till all hours."

James looked at Laura. *Ever since she found the bracelet she's changed,* he thought. The Laura he trusted and loved was dissolving. She was concealing something. He had to find out what it was and to do that he would have to be as devious as she was harsh. He'd have to start by finding this Merta.

"Could you show me where you found the bracelet?" James asked casually. Probably she'd met the girl by the river.

Laura crossed her legs and stared thoughtfully at the ground. There were some of last year's peach stones and the cap of a beer bottle lying under the table. They were so trivial, so typical of this world, where she had to live separated by vast distances of time from Loen, while in another world Merta was living under a curse. She sighed and looked up the valley where the green mountains turned into a rim of cliffs. A shadow was drifting over them. She heard the squawk of chickens. *I suppose there's no harm in that,* she thought.

"All right," she said. "I'll take you there this afternoon."

"I found the bracelet over there, just beyond that stone with the white band."

Laura pointed to the place. She and James were lying on their stomachs in the mossy shadow of the trees edging the river which flashed and rippled in the sun.

James leaned his chin in his hands and peered through the fringe of leaves at the stone solid against the milky green river.

"How do you suppose it got there?"

Laura did not answer. She was staring at the gap in the cliff on the other side of the river. Merta had first seen Tural there. He must have come down the mountain on the opposite side of the valley.

"What do you think?"

Laura hardly heard James's prompting question. She wanted to cross the river, to see if there was any trace of Tural, any clue which would tell her if Loen had removed the curse Flear had put on the bracelet and the golden collar.

"I want to cross the river," she said, getting up suddenly. "I don't think we'll use the ford."

"What ford?" James said in a surprised voice.

"Nothing."

Laura wondered how she could cross to the other side. There was only one way. They would have to climb the rocks at the head of the pool and jump across the fall.

"I can't see why you want to go up there," James said. The only thing he wanted to do was to find Merta and discover why Laura had changed so in the last two days. Climbing a mountain wouldn't help him.

"Because I must. You needn't come."

"Of course I will."

He followed her to the head of the pool and they began the climb up the great boulder. The stone gritted their fingers and grazed their knees as they pulled themselves puffing and gasping to the top. The river sluiced between the boulders as smooth as poured treacle, heavy with the power it gathered in its fall from the mountain.

Laura hesitated, then jumped and landed on hands and knees. She waited for James and then pushed her way through the bushes on top of the cliff till she came to the gap. The stream trickled over a bed of gravel to join the river.

She looked up and caught her breath. There was an overgrown track just visible, following the course of the stream up through the forest. At one time it would have been wide enough for horses.

"What do we do now?" James asked.

"Go up there."

"I think you're mad."

"Stay here then. I've told you you needn't come."

Laura was looking at him with eyes so intent, so filled with knowledge she would not share with him James had to follow her.

The mountainside was very steep and all the time the stream bore to the left. Soon they could not hear the river and the stream made only the faintest sound. Laura forced her way along the remnants of the track snaking through the trees over ground snared with brambles and slippery with pine needles.

As they climbed the stream grew weaker and weaker till it was first a thread thinly trickling from one stone to the next, then a succession of little pools the size of washbasins, and then it dried up altogether and they were walking beside a dry bed which would only ring with the sound of water after storms.

At last the spaces between the trees became wider and less matted with brambles. Their legs were burning from scratches and their hands were sticky with resin from dragging themselves up the slope by holding onto branches.

"Look at this!" Laura shouted. She pulled herself around

a tree trunk and stood on a well-trodden path. "We've climbed all this way and now there's a path."

There was no sign of the track she had followed from the river going further up the mountain. She was bitterly disappointed.

"Paths have a habit of going to places," James said encouragingly as Laura picked some wood sorrel and started chewing the leaves. "Let's follow it and see what we find."

Laura stalked up the path with James walking behind her. He could see no point in what she was doing, but he felt he had to humor her. Aimlessly climbing the mountain, he thought, was just one more example of Laura's odd, unpredictable behavior.

"It stops." Laura's voice brought James back to the path and the heat.

Sometime in the winter a landslide had roared down the mountain, uprooting trees and scouring away the earth with an abrasive shower of stones. The path disappeared under a great mound edged with a band of gray melting snow.

Laura had reached the crest of the slide and was slithering down the other side when she saw the second path. It was very faint, a crushed blade of grass, a bush with the leaves brushed back to show their undersides. These were the only traces. It began at the base of the landslide and went straight up the mountain. After about fifty meters it disappeared around a shoulder of rock. She was certain it was the continuation of the track Tural had followed to reach the river.

Laura started the climb.

James found her standing in a grassy clearing like a shelf

cut out of the side of the mountain. The path could go no further.

Laura was looking moodily around. The shelf was about three meters across, and a blown-down spruce tree lay covering most of it. Grass as fine as green hair thrust through the dead branches. The torn roots stuck up like the legs of a sun-dried crab. Behind the roots was a low cliff of ferny rock. She wondered why someone had started to chop up the tree and then stopped.

James pushed his way between the tree and the cliff. He had forgotten his quest for Merta. He wanted to examine that part of a spruce which is normally buried under the ground to see how the trunk turned into roots.

Laura watched him disappear behind the roots as he stooped down to get a better look.

The sun coming through the trees was hot on her shoulders and she looked up into a clear blue sky streaked with the trail of a jet flying south. Her attention drifted from James. *I'll never find anything,* she thought. *I'll never know what happened to the collar.*

"Laura!" James called urgently. "Come here, quick."

9 ‡ Iron Fragment

There was a low cave opening in the side of the mountain.

"Come on," James said.

He crept into the opening. Laura followed. The cave could just hold them both. There was enough light for Laura to see that it was about two meters deep and that on a ledge behind James's head there were globs of candle wax. The air was cold and damp. She looked longingly at the patch of sunlight beyond the mouth.

James pointed at the roof. On the stone were black patches, soot thrown up by guttering candles. "Someone's been working here."

Laura whispered, "Do you think it was long ago?"

James shook his head and picked up an empty cigarette packet. It was blue and squashed flat and very muddy.

"Look at this," he said twisting around and pointing at

a hole about a foot and half square below the ledge which had been used to hold the candles.

"I'm not crawling in there," Laura said sharply.

"You can't. It only goes in about two feet."

James pulled a box of matches out of his pocket. A match spluttered and warm orange light fell on their faces. The hole was a black square in the glistening wall of rock. Laura compelled herself to put her hand inside.

"It's cold," she said, "and damp. Is there anything there?"

"I don't know," James shook the match to put it out. "Feel around and find out. There's only one match left."

Laura ran the tips of her fingers across the bottom of the hole. She touched something rough and hard. She whipped her hand back as if she had been stung.

James sensed the terror in her voice as she said, "Light the match, James!"

They peered with dazzled eyes into the hole.

"I can't see anything," James said.

"It's right at the back."

James reached into the hole.

"There it is." Laura pointed over his shoulder.

The flame touched James's fingers as he picked up what Laura had seen.

He dropped the match hurriedly. The flame wilted, but before it died Laura saw that the match lay in the print of a hobnailed boot.

Laura glanced over her shoulder in case the owner of the boot blocked the cave mouth.

"Someone's been here recently."

"He smokes cigarettes." James sucked his burnt fingers.

"What do you think he was doing?"

"How should I know. Come on, I want to see what this is."

James crawled back into the sunlight.

A scrap of rusty iron no bigger than a razor blade lay in the palm of his hand. The rust was making the iron flaky like puff pastry.

"What is it?" Laura asked, holding James's hand to stop it wobbling.

A gust of wind clattered through the trees and as the leaves shivered James let the fragment of iron drop into Laura's palm.

At once her face was dragged into a dreadful mask of pain. Her eyes were squeezed tight and her lips twisted back from her teeth. She threw her head in spasms from side to side and her hair flew out in a web.

She was like a witch at an ordeal by fire when she grasps the burning iron and finds her magic powerless. The flesh sears, the sinews shrivel.

"Laura!" James shouted in fright. "What's the matter, Laura?"

At that moment Laura screamed. Beneath the tangled web of hair her mouth gaped open like a wound. Her screams were the most terrifying sounds James had ever heard, as if a lance was being pushed slowly into her lungs.

Her voice tore through his brain. He wanted to press his hands to his head to shut out her torment, yet within the agony of her screams James knew she was trying to speak.

He shouted her name again. "Laura! Laura!"

"Take it out of my hand! Take it out!" Laura's mouth was wrenched sideways with the effort of speaking and her eyes were sightless with fear. "Open my hand!"

James clutched Laura's hand. Her fingers were closed like a trap. He tried to pull open the hinges of her knuckles but they tightened under his grip as if she was being made to resist him. He held her wrist with both his hands and shook her arm up and down.

"Let go!" he shouted at her. "Why don't you let go!"

He tried to prise his fingers under hers. She stared through him with eyes widened by horror. Dank lines of hair clung to her open lips. She cried out as he pushed his fingers into her palm and just touched the piece of rusty iron frozen there.

As the iron's edge crumbled beneath his nails a bitter, freezing wind swept around him and he smelt the stinging cold of snow.

Without warning Laura's hand went slack, snapped over, and the fragment of iron spun through the air and fell into a scattering of red scales at James's feet.

James saw Laura's palm. The impression of the iron was like a burn. She tilted her face to the sky and gasped for breath. Her eyes were closed and she moaned with pain as she slowly moved her hand, opening and closing her fingers.

James was as exhausted as if he had just run a long way up a steep hill. There was a rancid, coppery taste in his mouth.

"Oh, Laura, what was it?" a woman's voice said in French.

James spun around. Madame Boulard was standing by the tree. He had never been so glad to see a friend.

"Those terrible screams. Child, child!"

Laura was swaying on her feet. James caught her just as she was about to fall.

"Quick!" he said to Madame Boulard.

Together they half carried Laura to the edge of the clearing and laid her down with her back against the rock.

Laura opened her eyes and stared weakly at James and Madame Boulard. She brushed hair out of her eyes.

"I thought you were going to die." James knelt down and held her hand. "What was it, Laura?" He could still hear her screams.

Madame Boulard smoothed the hair on Laura's forehead.

"You're safe," she said gravely, "thank heaven for that."

"But what was the matter?" James had to understand. "Why did you scream so?" He turned to Madame Boulard. "She couldn't open her hand."

"It was all so dark and cold," Laura said weakly. "I saw someone being killed. I could hear everything."

"Everything? You are sure?" Madame Boulard turned away.

"Oh, yes."

"What was she holding, James?" Madame Boulard asked.

Instantly James knew that the iron fragment had been a sword. "A piece of iron, we found it in there." He pointed. "There's a little cave hidden behind those roots."

Laura slowly stood up and put her hand on the rock to support herself.

"How did you know we were here?"

"Don't tire yourself, Laura." Madame Boulard tried to hold Laura's arm.

"How did you know?" Laura asked again. She snatched her arm away.

"I was walking up the path from the valley and saw you. I followed you and heard you screaming. That's all, Laura." Madame Boulard turned to James. "Have you been here before?"

"No," James said. "Someone else has though. We saw footprints in the cave."

"What were they like?" Madame Boulard asked sharply.

"Hobnailed boots. There was a cigarette packet in there too." But James was more interested in the cause of Laura's fear. "Who was it you saw, Laura?"

"I don't know." Laura was about to burst into tears. "I want to get away from here. I hate this place."

She walked unsteadily toward the path.

Madame Boulard gave James a look which ordered him to stop questioning Laura. He was surprised by the unexpected determination in her face.

"Perhaps I should tell you a little more about myself," Madame Boulard said as though she were trying to take his thoughts from Laura. She paused while they walked slowly down to the landslide.

She went on, "Every now and then, if I hold a piece of metal, or a bit of cloth, anything, something strange happens."

They reached the landslide and started to cross it.

"Let me explain it to you," Madame Boulard said as they regained the path on the other side. "You know when you shut your eyes and try to see a very familiar place, your bedroom perhaps, or when you try to remember the sound of someone's voice. You know how confused it all becomes. You see part of a bed in darkness, or a chair. It's like looking at blurry photographs. And you can't really remember someone's voice, can you? You only see little bits of the whole picture and hear little scraps of sound."

James shut his eyes and tried to see his bedroom. Madame Boulard was right. He saw the table beside the bed in a murk, he couldn't make the lamp or the pile of books come sharply into focus.

"It's like that," Madame Boulard went on, "when I hold things. I see faint pictures and hear confused sounds. I have a little Greek lamp at home—you know how fascinated I am by the past—it's over two thousand years old. I was holding it once and saw the corner of a room and heard two people talking. I think they were quarrelling. Is that what happened to you, Laura, when you held that piece of iron?"

Laura walked on without answering. Then she said evasively, "It was rather."

"Do you know what the piece of iron was?" Madame Boulard asked.

"I think it was part of a sword," James said.

Laura stopped. "What?" she demanded.

"I don't know how I know, it frightened me."

"Perhaps," Madame Boulard said, "it was because you were holding Laura's hand."

James remembered standing with her in the garden and the way she had put her thumbs over his wrists to make the wire move. *It must have been that,* he thought, *only this time I was holding Laura's hand when she saw someone being killed.* He gripped Laura's arm. "Who was it you saw?"

"I couldn't tell."

"Try and remember, please, Laura."

"It was just a face." Laura shivered uncontrollably.

"Laura," Madame Boulard said thoughtfully, "could it have been this girl your bracelet shows you?"

"What do you mean," James said desperately. "What girl does the bracelet show you, Laura?"

"I don't just see things." Laura looked resentfully at Madame Boulard. "I'm actually there. I become Merta."

James looked at Laura uneasily.

"Don't be angry with me, Laura," Madame Boulard said. The muscles in her face were tense. "You know what I'm trying to do for you."

Madame Boulard walked on down the path. When they could hear the river Madame Boulard stopped and turned to face James and Laura. She was standing on the soft loamy hump of a mole's tunnel running across the path.

"I expect you'll be going home that way," she said pointing down the mountain.

"But where does this path go to?" James asked.

"Into the valley. It goes past a farm and comes out near the village. Some people say there used to be a mule track the way you're going which crossed the river at a ford, though I've never seen a trace of it."

She walked away from them and then came hurriedly back.

"Laura," she said earnestly, "do you think your bracelet would show me Merta?"

"No," Laura said bluntly.

"You could lend it to me the next time you come for a lesson."

Laura noticed an intense, hungry look in Madame Boulard's eyes. *I wish I'd never told her,* she thought bitterly. *I shouldn't have told anyone.*

"Yes," Laura said distantly.

"How can I possibly set your mind at rest if you won't let me see the bracelet, Laura?" Madame Boulard paused as if she was searching for a way of persuading Laura. Then she said, "But I must warn you. Some things bring their past with them. This girl died hundreds of years ago. You must live as Laura."

She touched Laura lightly on the arm and hurried away along the path.

"If I were you, I should lend the bracelet to Madame Boulard," James said, kicking a stone. "Then it will be out of the house and you won't have to worry about Julian."

"Do you think she's telling the truth?"

"What about?"

"Seeing us on the path and following us to the cave." Laura's voice was quick, panicky. "She might have been hanging about looking for the place where I found the bracelet. She could have trailed us from the river!"

"Nonsense!" James turned to face Laura. "Tell me everything about this girl Merta."

"No, James, there's Mother and Julian."

"If I said you held a piece of iron and saw someone murdered centuries ago, do you think they'd believe me?"

"I can't risk it, James."

"Well, you're not stopping me finding out how the bracelet makes you become this girl. If it does."

"We stood Aunt Lydia together, James. Give me a bit more time."

She couldn't forget the hungry look in Madame Boulard's eyes, or her insistence that Laura lend her the bracelet. Madame Boulard was interested in the past. Everything stable was crumbling around Laura. No faces told the truth, she hardly dared look at James.

James thought for a moment. "All right, Laura," he said, "but you could at least trust me." He glanced at his sister. She was wan, her body was like a husk surrounding nothing, her eyes just openings into emptiness. "I hate that bracelet!"

Laura pushed her hands wildly through her hair and ran to the river.

10 ‡ *Gian's Rocks*

It was a brilliantly sunny morning and a waning moon hung white as a ghost above the mountains to the west.

James sat on the front doorstep and watched Laura. She was standing under the walnut trees and staring up at the moon.

James was tormented by the warning Madame Boulard had given Laura on their walk down the mountain, and he could not forget the struggle to open Laura's hand. *There's no point in talking to Laura about it,* he thought, *she'll just look at me as if she doesn't know who I am.*

He shivered despite the sun and wished Laura would leave the world the bracelet showed her and come back to his world of dusty feet in sandals and the smell of warm grass and the sound of the river coming up from the valley. *If only I knew more about the bracelet,* he thought. *I must bring her back, stop her turning into a person she's not meant to be.*

He heard his mother.

"James," she called. "Julian and I are going to the office in Geneva. We'll be back for supper, be sensible, look after yourselves."

James was thinking too intently about Laura's bracelet to really hear what his mother said to him. He heard the click of her heels as she walked up to the barn.

Julian! Of course! Julian would know about Laura's bracelet. James was furious with himself for not thinking this before. *I don't care what I promised Laura. I'll ask Julian.*

He leapt to his feet and dashed around the house. He heard the car back out of the barn. He reached it just as Julian was driving up the track.

James caught hold of the door handle and ran panting beside the car.

"Julian," he shouted, "wait a minute."

Julian slammed on the brakes. His sunglasses stared blankly at James.

"What do you want, James? We're in a hurry."

"The bracelet . . ." James didn't know where to start; he only saw Julian's blank staring glance and heard the engine revving angrily. "Do you know anything about bracelets?"

"What kind of bracelets?"

"Old ones . . ."

"For heaven's sake, James, there's bound to be a book in my study."

Julian let in the clutch with a bang. James stood watching the car surge up the track to the road, the fat tires squelching over the gravel.

His mother put her hand out of the window and fluttered her fingers at him briefly; then they were gone.

Laura was still watching the waning moon grow transparent in the brilliant blue sky. It was slowly disappearing, dissolving, thinning with light.

She sat down and leaned her back against one of the walnut trees. Now that her mother and Julian had driven off, she took the bracelet out of her pocket and put it on her wrist, slipping it up her forearm. For the first time she noticed a thin white circle like a scar on her tanned skin, just below the elbow. She touched it. The skin was numb. She couldn't feel her fingers touching the white mark. Her hands were trembling as she touched the mark again. She could feel nothing.

The waning moon was drawing her away from the valley as it was dragging Merta away. She was weak and sweating with fear. In only a few more days the moon would die.

The sunlight blazed mockingly on the gold; shadows of walnut leaves fluttered over it. The eyes stared fiercely at her. Even though the leaves were barely stirring a cold wind was wrapping itself around her shoulders. She heard horses moving through the valley. For an instant the sun blinked.

She was riding beside Loen and they were passing the ford across the river where they had met Tural.

"How far is it?" she asked.

"Nearly a day's ride."

Sethor jogged behind them leading a pack horse.

A few hours ago she had seen Flear and Tural escaping from Loen's hall. At dawn Loen had ordered horses saddled for a journey.

"We're going to Gian," Loen had told her as she mounted her horse in the half-light before the sun rose. "He's the only one who can help us."

"What'll he do to me?" She tried to sound as if she didn't care.

"I don't know, Merta." Loen reached up and held her face between his hands. He drew her down and kissed her.

Merta changed the grip on the reins to ease the aching pain of the bracelet on her arm. The golden collar was tight and heavy around her neck. Arne had betrayed her. All along he had been in league with Flear and Tural. The words he spoke in his own language as he dropped the plaited straw on the molds had prepared the bracelet and the collar to receive Flear's curse.

A biting wind poured down from the mountains and the sky was a clear white lit by a dim sun. She wriggled her shoulders further into the heavy cloak of beaver skins Loen had put around her before they left his hall.

The path they followed cut through the wood of black trees hanging with icicles. Soon the valley opened out and the path was wider, more clearly defined through the hummocky, snow-covered undergrowth.

The mountains were falling back, becoming less wild. They rode all morning, too oppressed by the weight of Flear's curse to talk. At midday they halted for a hurried meal, then rode on as the hard winter sun dropped lower and lower in the sky. At last they turned south and climbed a stony pass between two peaks of bare yellow rock streaked with snow.

At the top of the pass they paused for a moment. Merta gazed down at a huge frozen lake ringed by mountains. Flurries of snow driven by the wind darted across the ice.

"We're nearly there," Loen said encouragingly.

He kicked his horse on. A few minutes later he veered off the track they had followed all day. They were riding along a narrow ledge striking across the face of one of the mountains flanking the pass.

Loen pointed ahead. "There's Gian's Rocks."

Two enormous black rocks stuck out from the mountain. Between them was a low wooden hut. Merta saw a girl standing in the doorway staring at the riders coming toward her.

The girl threw something into the snow and disappeared into the hut.

"That's Gian's daughter," Loen told her.

They dismounted in the sunless gloom under the rocks which hung right over the hut like a huge roof of stone. The rocks were covered in moss and bearded with tufts of withered frozen grass.

Merta noticed a mess of bones lying in the snow. *So that's what Gian's daughter was doing,* she thought as she pulled the cloak tight around her shoulders and let Sethor tie up her horse. She looked up at the rocks and felt giddy. They seemed to be moving through the sky, about to fall on her and crush her to a smear.

A raven was circling overhead. It came lower and lower. She watched it alight and walk stiffly toward the bones sticking up in the snow. Its wings were violet black, the eyes sharp with life. She longed to be the bird and not herself, to change her arm crippled by the bracelet and her

neck gripped by the collar for the pure beauty of the
raven's wings and the darting movement of its beak.

But Loen was leading her into the hut and making her
sit on a stool by the fire.

The hut was warm and stuffy and smelled of greasy
cooking. There were blobs of gray fat on the hearthstone
and two wooden bowls were lying in the ashes. Gian's
daughter was standing in the shadows.

Merta guessed the girl was a bit younger than herself.
She was slatternly and plump with two plaits of lank hair
lying over her shoulders. She looked nervously from Loen
to Merta.

"Where's your father?" Loen asked.

"Fetching wood."

Gian's daughter hung back from the fire. Merta saw the
girl's eyes darting anxiously from side to side.

"Don't be frightened of us," Loen said, "you've seen me
before." He moved toward the girl. "We've only come to
ask for your help."

"But he'll need me. He always needs me when men like
you come here."

She put her hands to her face and Merta heard her sobbing and snivelling. The girl turned away from them and
cowered against the wall.

Suddenly the door was kicked open and a fat little man
staggered in under a load of faggots. He threw them down
on the floor and stared at Loen and Merta. His eyes were
almost hidden in fat and there were great rolls of fat
around his wrists making his hands look small and deli-
cate. He wiped his runny nose on the back of his hand and
sat down heavily on a stool close to Merta.

"Well, Loen," Gian said breathing heavily. "What do you want now? I saw you last when your father died. You didn't take my advice then."

Loen walked swiftly across the hut and stood in front of Gian.

"Last night Flear put a curse on Merta."

"And Arne worked it too," Merta said.

Gian's beady little eyes sparkled.

"Stop dribbling and snivelling, girl," he shouted at his daughter. "Maybe I won't need you at all." He looked intently at Merta. "So you're the one Loen brought to his hall. Do your mother and father know what Flear's done?"

"They're dead." Loen took her hand and spoke for her. "They pledged Merta to me when my father was alive."

Gian pulled a stick from one of the faggots and threw it on the fire.

"And what did Flear do?" he asked, as if he wasn't really interested.

"Flear cursed the gold I gave Merta when she came to me."

"Who made it?"

"A smith called Arne. Tural sent him."

Gian tossed another stick onto the fire.

"You trusted him!"

"He was only a goldsmith."

Gian was holding a stick across his knees.

"You trust people too much, Loen. You're brave and rich and men want to cheat you."

He leaned forward poking the fire and looking out of the corners of his eyes at Merta. "What kind of curse, Loen?"

"The gold can't be taken from her and she wanes with the moon."

Gian pursed his lips. "How did Flear lay it?"

"She sang with a harp. She came as an old woman begging shelter."

"I forget how young you are, Loen, and that's why you always want help from Gian who lives with his daughter in a hut like a pig pen. Show me the gold, Merta."

Reluctantly Merta drew her arm from under the cloak and pulled back the sleeve of her dress.

Gian sucked his teeth and bent forward till his fat cheeks almost touched Merta's arm. She flinched when he put his forefinger on the bracelet.

"Plaited wheat," he said softly. "Let me see the collar."

Merta pulled the cloak away from her neck.

"Wheat again," Gian said, "and the same face between the ears."

"What can we do, Gian?" Loen's voice was despairing.

"I can tell you, but it may not save her."

He pointed a stabbing finger at his daughter.

"Get me some snow, girl."

They all looked at Gian's daughter. She was hiding her face with her hands and sobbing uncontrollably. Merta could see the tears dripping through her grubby fingers.

"Hurry, girl, or I'll lay this on you." Gian threatened her with the stick.

She took a few shuffling paces toward the door.

"I can't, Father!" Her voice was a wail of protest. She dropped her hands helplessly to her side. Her face was drawn with fear. "I don't want to see them. I don't want to see those things."

Merta jumped up and put her arms around the girl's shoulders. She felt her shuddering and quaking. She looked at Gian.

"Must she?" Merta pleaded.

"You want to live, don't you?" Gian said placidly.

Merta found the girl looking into her eyes. She had stopped crying. Her face was shining with tears. Without saying anything she hurried out of the hut.

"She always does this now," Gian said. "Doesn't mean a thing."

He waddled over to a shelf fixed near the door and picked up a small square of black slate.

"Sit down both of you," he said quietly, "and don't make a sound."

His daughter came back carrying a lump of snow.

"That's better," Gian coaxed her. "You know what to do."

The girl sat on a stool opposite Gian and put the lump of snow on the slate Gian was holding on his knees.

Gian bent forward and breathed on his daughter's eyes.

Merta saw the lashes flutter, the eyelids close. The girl was rocking backward and forward. Then her hands started moving over the snow. Her fingers were red and puffy with cold. They began molding the snow, rapidly, deftly, making the effigy of a woman, a thick snow body and a round snow head.

She began to moan and her hands clutched convulsively. The moaning grew louder, more intensely sad. A column of sound grew above the snow figure.

The hair pricked on Merta's neck.

The sound thickened, became voices. Merta heard a woman laughing behind her. She spun around to see who had come into the hut. There was no one there. A jibbering cackle came from above her. Merta wanted to run out of the hut, hurl herself down the mountain to the frozen water of the lake. Do anything to escape.

Then she heard Flear's unmistakeable sweet voice singing wild and clear.

The song changed to a drowning sob. A drop of water trickled down from the head of snow and ran across the slate.

Gian was blowing on his daughter's eyes. He put his mouth close to her ear and whispered. "How shall I release the gold?"

Flear cried to them, "Arne or death." Her voice was cracking, she was gnawed by pain.

Gian whispered, "What stays the gold?"

Flear's answer was a scream. Water was dripping from the snow in thin streams.

"What stays the gold?" Gian asked again.

Flear was moaning, cursing, yelling in a voice so wracked they could only just make out her words, "Bury one, drown one."

Gian's mouth was close to his daughter's motionless lips. "Who finds the gold?"

The air shook with the torment in Flear's voice. It was a voice from a body torn and crushed.

"Must do what Loen must do."

Gian spoke once more, "What cures the gold?"

Flear was whimpering. The voice was falling, wilting, thinning out, shaping one word, "Death."

The snow crumbled on the slate, water dribbled onto the floor. The voice became a wail hanging over their heads, trailing into silence.

Merta dragged her gaze from the little heap of melting snow and looked at Gian's daughter. Her eyes were still closed, her chest was rising and falling and her forehead was beaded with sweat. Her eyelids fluttered and opened.

A wide, stupid smile spread across her face.

Gian patted her on the knee.

"Good girl," he said, "that was a good girl."

He leaned across Merta and whispered to Loen, "She'll remember what happened to her in the morning, where she's been and what she saw, then she won't look so happy."

"Do you know what I should do?" Loen asked impatiently.

Gian looked thoughtfully at the black slate balanced on his knees.

"Arne put a blessing on the gold, that's why the wheat's there. He can take the collar and the bracelet from Merta." Gian paused. "If you can find him."

Merta couldn't believe what she heard.

"But he rode away with Tural!"

"Did you see if he was bound?"

Gian's question cut Merta to the heart. She remembered the way Tural had brought Arne to the river bank bound to his horse, and Arne's voice muttering over the plait of burning straw. She loved Arne for the beauty of what he made and the unbending way he endured his fate. She hated herself for doubting him.

"Don't you know more?" Loen demanded.

"If you can't find Arne you must kill Flear." Gian pointed his finger at the bracelet and the collar. "Those won't cling to Merta when Flear's dead." He chuckled. "Nor when Merta's dead. They'll fall off like leaves then."

Loen stepped angrily toward Gian. "What about the gold?"

Gian stared at the pool of water on the slate.

"What shall I do with the gold?" Loen asked again.

"You must hide it. That curse won't be broken till it's claimed a life." Gian wiped the back of his hand across his mouth. "You must bury the collar and drown the bracelet, for if one is found the other will be and whoever has the bracelet will know what Merta knows."

Loen was standing over Gian.

"So killing Flear or finding Arne won't break the curse."

"No. That bracelet and collar can be made to fall from Merta, and they won't cling to anyone again. They'll claim a life though if they're not drowned and buried when the moon wanes. Once they've killed they'll be as harmless as the little piece of gold you could pay me for what I've told you."

Gian looked up at Loen and a self-satisfied smile puckered his fat greasy face.

Loen's patience snapped.

"Where are Arne and Flear?" He was shaking Gian like a bag of blubber.

Gian pushed Loen away.

"I can't read the future, Loen." Gian waved his hand to show Loen the difficulty of finding two people in the immensity of the forest. "Can you count the trees hiding them?"

Gian tilted up the slate, letting a stream of water run onto the floor.

Loen was so young, and the task was so great. There was so little time, only four days to the first moonless night.

11 ‡ *Col Depraz*

James stood in the doorway of Julian's study and wondered where to begin his search.

He had once read about the Collier brothers in New York, two old men who had completely filled their house with paper. Julian's study was like one of the Colliers' rooms. Papers were everywhere. Piles of newspapers on the floor, bulging Manila folders, brown wallets tied with faded pink ribbon, boxes of typing paper and envelopes, stacks of notebooks.

If he moved he was sure a pile of books or a pyramid of newspapers would avalanche and he would have to waste time putting it back.

He threaded his way to the bookcase which ran along one wall. He saw books on New Guinea, prehistoric

Europe, Greece, Rome, Turkey. A great many were written in German or Italian and James could not even translate the titles.

He compelled himself to look along every shelf for a reassuring title. There was a pile of new books about Celtic art and Hittite pottery, but nowhere a good simple title like *Gold Bracelets*.

He shut his eyes and pulled a book at random from the shelves. He found he was holding a copy of *Level IX at Ulk al Hrupta* written by Sir Latham Minty-Coacher, M.A., D.Litt., etc., etc. The book was bound in scuffed paper and looked extremely dull. Julian must have found it fascinating; every page bore comments in his very neat, very spidery writing.

James snapped the book shut and angrily pushed Sir Latham Minty-Coacher's account of how he spent the summer of 1927 back into the shelf.

He left the bookcase and stood in front of the desk. Its surface was as cluttered as the floor. On either side of the electric typewriter there were piles of Manila folders; three Dundee marmalade pots bristled with pencils and ballpoint pens.

James felt utterly defeated. It would take him years to read through all the books, a century.

In despair his attention wandered to the typewriter. He stared blindly at the bossy black keys. Then he noticed the corner of a folder just sticking out from under the typewriter.

Why did Julian shove that under there, he thought. Very gingerly, so as not to move anything else, James inched out the folder. On the cover Julian had written NAVIER RE. GOLD.

James snatched it up, looked through it, and ran to find Laura.

She was still gazing blindly at the moon which was now nearly washed away by sunlight.

"Laura, look at this!"

He pushed the folder into her hands.

She twisted her head quickly from side to side in a spasm, as if she'd been in a deep sleep and he'd acted like some unwelcome alarm clock.

"Come on, Laura—look. Can't you see, it says GOLD."

Laura dragged herself away from the reek of Gian's hut. She stared at the vast landscape of mountains and forest. She was sure Loen could never find Arne or Flear.

She dimly heard James asking her to look at something. Laura moved her arm. Sunlight flashed on the bracelet and the white mark below her elbow stung as if it had been tied with nettles. She was opening a folder, seeing words in Julian's writing.

She read: "15th May. Went to Col Depraz at Paccot's unexpected request. Saw quite unique and beautiful piece. Just what Navier's been wanting for years. Telephoned Paris. Navier arrives Annecy day after tomorrow. Professor Nalgo, the conceited jackass, will have the devil's own job saying when and where this one was made. Paccot most distrustful, refused to let me take it away with me. Thinks it safer in his shed than my bank. Perhaps he's right!"

Laura idly turned the paper over. There was a polaroid photograph clipped on the back.

"There it is!" James shouted breathlessly. "It's what Julian's selling. He doesn't want your bracelet at all."

The day shrunk around Laura as her whole being con-

centrated on the photograph. She was looking at the collar
Arne had made.

"Oh, James . . ." Laura sprang to her feet. Her eyes
were blazing.

"We must go to Col Depraz," she said. "I must get that
collar."

She was certain she had only to bury the collar and
throw her bracelet back into the river to release herself
from Flear's curse.

James found Col Depraz on a large scale map and was
intrigued by another discovery. The path they had taken to
the landslide led up to the col. On the contours marking
the summit was a little black dot, a shed.

It was midday when they crossed the landslide. A kilo-
meter farther on the forest gave way to tussocky grass.
Laura strode on ahead looking neither to right nor to left,
following the path which snaked up the mountain as if she
was being drawn to the col by an invisible thread.

James panted after her, occassionally stopping to take a
drink from his wineskin which he had filled from one of
the bottles of *vin ordinaire* in the kitchen while Laura put
the bracelet into its hiding place.

As they climbed higher they heard the dull clink clank
of cowbells, and coming to a lip where the ground became
less steep they saw the cows grazing beside a stream. The
cows were a deep chestnut color and their flanks were
scaled with mud. Twitching their ears, they tore the grass,
chewing it with long trails of spittle hanging from their
mouths.

"How much farther?" James called to Laura. The wine
made him feel incredibly hot.

"Not far." Laura didn't even turn her head but kept on, almost running toward the col.

At last they raced up a gentle incline and knew they had reached the top. The col was a saddle of grass between two ragged mountains which rose on either side. In front of James and Laura was a fringe of grass bent over by the wind. There was no sign of a shed.

"Look!"

Laura had seen the ridge of a corrugated iron roof poking above the fringe of grass.

They ran the last few yards and stopped.

"Look at that!" they both said together, but James and Laura were looking at two different things.

James was staring at a far distant horizon. He no longer felt tired. There, lying below a band of cloud, were the high Alps—mile upon mile of jumbled, infinitely distant snow rising to a smooth brilliantly white summit. He was seeing Mont Blanc for the first time.

"Mont Blanc, Laura!" James said as if he was in a trance.

"Never mind Mont Blanc. There's Paccot's shed."

James pulled his eyes from the mountains.

From where they stood the ground sloped steeply and then flattened out for a hundred meters before falling into a valley with houses no bigger than specks on a map and traced with a road winding into a village. Tucked against the slope was an ancient, sinister looking shed which had been reroofed with corrugated iron. The ground nearby was all brown mud, dry, but pocked by cow's feet and spattered with greeny black cow pats.

Laura ran down the slope. She passed a low window masked with dust and cobwebs. Around the corner was a door and in the slope of the roof a round hole with smoke, paled by sunlight, flickering from its lip.

The door was shut.

Laura banged her clenched fist on the weather-beaten wood.

"Nobody will hear that," James said, "the door hasn't even rattled."

"I'll see if it's unlocked."

She lifted the latch. The door swung open.

Laura and James looked into the most archaic room they had ever seen. A fire smoldered under a huge copper cauldron hanging from a chain. A flurry of smoke curled around the belly of the cauldron and up through the hole in the roof. There was not even a chimney to guide the smoke within the room. Two narrow stools were pulled out from a rough table. The end of a loaf and a knife lay on the bare wood.

Laura walked impulsively into the dimly lit room while James stayed by the door. Her eyes darted around. *Where does he keep it,* she asked herself, *he must have hidden it somewhere.* She looked up at the ceiling. The rafters were black from years of smoke. Two beams stretched across the room and on top of them lay billets of firewood, pine split with an axe. Under the cauldron a great pile of wood ash spread over the floor. A pool of milk sweated and steamed, yellow within the spotlessly clean copper.

"No one's here," James said apprehensively. "Shouldn't we go home?"

Laura was about to answer when they heard a noise. They jerked around to face the door.

A man stood there. He was enormously tall, frightening, with a face stubbled with black hairs against dark sun-browned skin. His nose was sharply prominent and curved like a blade. His huge fists were clenching at his side. Narrow eyes glared at them.

Swiftly and soundlessly he shut the door.

"What do you want?" he asked.

Without taking his eyes off them the man pulled a polished iron key out of his pocket and turned the lock. He reached up to a beam beyond their reach and hung the key on a peg. As he moved they heard the nails in his boots grating on the stone floor.

"Who told you to come here?" He sat down on one of the stools.

He picked up the loaf and the knife. Laura watched the knife cut through the bread—it was sharp as a razor.

"Did your stepfather send you?" The man's voice was accusing.

"No!" Laura shouted.

"Do you think I don't know where you come from?"

Laura's eyes were fixed on his hands. He was squeezing a piece of bread between the nails of his thumb and forefinger. He was so powerful there was no chance of taking the collar by force. Once she'd found it she'd have to be cunning, counter his strength with guile.

"Sit down, both of you."

He lifted the other stool and cracked it down close to his own.

"You," he pointed at Laura, "sit here," and he stabbed the knife at the end of the stool nearest him. "Do you know what I do here?"

Laura sat down. "No," she said, unable to quite mask the fear in her voice.

"I make cheese, that's all. When the snow melts, I bring the cows and goats up from the valley and make cheese." He pointed at the cauldron. "Your stepfather told you my name's Paccot, didn't he. He's told you, hasn't he."

Laura wondered how to answer Paccot. Perhaps if she showed him she knew he had the collar there'd be much less cause to hide it from her.

"He's told us a little," she said, giving Paccot a rather false smile. "He spends most of his time dealing with a man who wants to buy something of yours."

"So you know that much, do you?" Paccot sucked his teeth and put another lump of bread into his mouth. He looked suspiciously at Laura, trying to fathom her.

"It must be terribly valuable," she said.

She sensed Paccot wavering. One more gentle push was all he needed.

James was feeling hot and thirsty. He still had some wine left. *I suppose I should offer Paccot a drink first,* he thought. Rather apprehensively, he gave him the wineskin.

Paccot looked surprised, but he unscrewed the stopper and took a long, steady squeeze. When he handed the wineskin back to James he smiled.

"Not bad, a little sweet—not bad at all," he said. "Maybe I'll show you something."

Laura wanted to hug James. Quite unconsciously, with one simple gesture, he had achieved everything she was striving for. She gripped the edge of the stool to control the trembling in her hands.

Paccot went to a dark corner of the room and Laura

heard a door open. She listened to his boots grate over stone as he moved about in the back of the shed. He came back carrying a cat. Laura's heart sank.

The cat was twice as big again as Matthieu's. It was striped like a smoky tiger. Flat ears stuck out at the side of its head and its yellow eyes glowed. Shining white claws prodded the leather sleeve of Paccot's coat.

To hide her disappointment, Laura reached out to stroke the cat's fur. Instantly it sprang at her hand.

"She's fierce," Paccot said proudly. "If anyone went into my store when I wasn't here, they wouldn't come out again. She's better than a dog."

He roughly scratched the cat's ears.

Laura considered what Paccot had said. He wouldn't keep a fierce cat in a store if there was nothing for it to guard. She had to be direct.

"I suppose you keep it in there," she said bluntly.

Paccot dropped the cat on the floor. He gazed at Laura for a moment and then, as if he were speaking to himself, said, "They're only children." Then he added, "Come with me."

He lit a candle stuck with a blob of wax onto a chipped blue enamel plate.

They followed Paccot into a long narrow room. On either side were shelves and on the shelves were rows and rows of cheeses, dusty pink in the candlelight. Paccot patted them possessively.

Laura's chest tightened. The collar must be hidden in the store, but she couldn't think where. She was surrounded by cheese, there was nothing but cheese, the air was thick with the smell of cheese. Then she saw the cat sitting inside a wooden crate and licking its fur.

"She sleeps there," Paccot said.

They stood around the crate and looked down at the cat. She had an old blanket felted over with molted hairs.

Paccot put the candle on a shelf. Unexpectedly he reached under the blanket and pulled out a cardboard box which he put beside the candle. The box had once held soap; the lid was decorated with the picture of a highly polished baby.

Paccot opened the box.

"There," he said proudly.

Laura was staring into a curving, twisting mesh of gold. Paccot's dark hand eclipsed the brilliant light.

"Take it," he said and roughly pushed the gold into Laura's hands. "Don't you want to see it?"

Laura shut her eyes, not daring to look at the collar. She felt her fingers move delicately over its surface. She felt the roundness of a face, the ridge of golden eyebrows, the sightless eyes. She remembered it around Merta's neck, the oppressive choking weight. She opened her eyes and caught her breath.

All the intricate molding on the collar glittered in the candle light. The ears of wheat swept around the face, each grain hard, perfect. The decoration was so sharp, so clear, the collar looked as if it had been worn only a few times. Laura realized how battered her bracelet was by comparison.

Just then Paccot lifted up the candle to light a cigarette which he took from a blue packet. Laura glanced at him.

"Where did you find it?" she asked, boldly holding the collar to her throat.

"In the forest near the landslide. There's a little cave there, luckily it's on my land."

Of course, Laura thought, *your hobnailed boots made those marks and it was your cigarette packet we saw on the ground.*

"A tree fell during the winter. When I went to chop it up a few days ago I found the cave." Paccot was rubbing his neck.

"There was nothing else?"

"An old bit of iron which I left there."

Laura's mind spun with questions and uncertain answers. The collar had been buried and the bracelet drowned, but that was no proof that Loen had found Arne or killed Flear and Tural.

For a second a burning pain swept around the faint white circle on her arm. The collar was growing heavier in her hands. Laura was convinced that before the moon waned she must bury the collar, but not in the cave, somewhere else where no one could dig it up again, and she must throw the bracelet into the deepest lake.

Sadness swept her. Without the bracelet she could never regain Merta, never know if Merta had grown old in Loen's hall. Still she could see Loen's hands trying to shake the truth out of Gian, his face tormented by the near impossibility of saving Merta. If she wanted to live as Laura as Madame Boulard urged her, she must cut herself off from Merta forever and that meant never being with Loen again.

Laura's hands were sweating as she turned the collar around. She was sickened by what she had to do. Paccot would never let her bury it. She had to steal it from him.

Her only chance was *now* with the collar locked in her hands. She must do something so unforeseen as to make Paccot and James unable to forestall her.

She must be quicker than light, run to the door, fly out

of the shed, race down the mountain and bury the collar in the forest.

"What's that?" she said, pointing to the back of the store.

As Paccot turned away from her, Laura hurled herself past James, zigzagged between the stools and the cauldron, wrenched at the latch.

The door was locked.

Paccot's hands slammed on her shoulders and spun her around. He tore the collar from her.

"Laura!" James's voice was shrill, accusing. Paccot had accepted Laura as innocent, guileless, shown them his treasure, shared James's wine.

Laura's face was white. She cowered before Paccot. He snatched the key from the beam and rammed it into the lock.

"Get out!" Paccot ripped open the door. "If you ever . . ." His voice trailed into silence as he shook the collar in Laura's face.

Why did she do it? James's mind ached with questions. *Why did she try and steal the collar? Could it be mixed up with the bracelet?* He heard Laura sobbing. Suddenly he remembered the last time he heard her cry. She was holding a fragment of iron. He was filled with dread. *Could that murder not be in the past but in the future?*

James ran past Paccot to the door.

12 ‡ Ball and String

"Where did you go this afternoon? Julian was terribly worried when we found you weren't here."

James's mother put a red earthenware bowl of spaghetti on the table. His heart sank. He was sure any food would make him sick. He hated spaghetti.

"Up a mountain," he replied vaguely. He never wanted anyone to know what Laura had done there. He felt ashamed and angry.

"I don't mind, but you could have left a message. Laura, Julian, supper's ready. Was it fun?"

"No, it wasn't."

They sat around the table. James handed plates to Laura and Julian and waited for his own.

His mother piled James's plate with a mound of spaghetti dripping with meat and tomato sauce. James drank some water to moisten his lips. He was still shocked from seeing Laura trying to steal Paccot's collar. She had refused to say a word to him on the walk home, isolating herself so he could not accuse her. All the time he was nagged by the thought that Laura's life could be in danger.

He looked at the food on his plate knowing exactly what was going to happen when he started to eat. Julian was twisting a fork in the bowl of a spoon to wind up an oozy, rusty-brown ball of spaghetti which he then put neatly into his mouth. Laura and his mother cut theirs demurely with the edge of a fork.

The spaghetti was like the day which had passed, all writhing and glutinuous, smeared with meat and garlic and sauce, as difficult to put into his mouth as it was to obliterate his memory of Paccot's face as he threw them out onto the col.

James picked up his knife and fork, harpooned the spaghetti and captured a long dripping mouthful, about two feet of which hung from his lips to his plate.

I knew it, James said to himself.

He tried to reel in the spaghetti with his tongue. It went in much too slowly and noisily, and he was aware that Julian had stopped eating to look at him. So he sucked. The spaghetti shot into his mouth. The last few inches flew between his lips, the ends whipped up and covered his nose with tomato and chopped onion.

"Must you eat like a pig?" Julian snapped. "If you're going to eat that way, cut it up."

James slashed the spaghetti but it only slithered about under the knife.

"Cut mouthfuls," Julian said disapprovingly.

Everyone else sat for five minutes in total silence in front of emptied plates while James finished his meal.

"Thank heaven that's over," Julian said gratefully as he poured himself a third glass of wine. "Which mountain did you climb?"

"We don't know its name," Laura said evasively, "we just went up the other side of the valley."

"You must be careful up there." Julian was twisting his glass around and looking intently at Laura.

"We were quite safe."

"You might think so, but these mountains are never safe. Mountains don't give second chances to the careless."

Laura fixed her eyes on Julian's. "We're not careless and we didn't get lost," she said, sticking out her chin.

"You might next time. I don't want local people risking their necks looking for you."

"I never thought you would," Laura said placidly. She watched Julian drink his wine.

Her mother put a dark blue plate on the table. There was a cheese on the plate.

"Look," Laura said. James heard shock in her voice.

The cheese was exactly like the ones they had seen in Paccot's store.

"What do you mean—look?" Julian asked.

"Nothing." Laura cut herself a small piece. Her mouth had suddenly gone dry and she found it difficult to swallow.

Julian reached hungrily across the table for the cheese. "If you've got something to say, say it, Laura."

Their mother said plaintively, "She's tired, Julian, after walking all that way."

"It's a very good cheese," Laura said. She remembered the strength of Paccot's hands on her shoulders.

"Do you know where it was made?"

"How could I."

"On the mountain you climbed today. We bought this one on our way home. If you'd climbed to the col you might have seen the man who made it, though I'm glad you didn't go that far."

"Why?" Laura asked.

Julian said nothing. Suddenly he pushed back his chair.

"I've got some work to do," he said from the door. "I must confirm those arrangements I made with Navier."

"I hate scolding you," their mother said as Julian walked upstairs to the study, "but he really does worry about you."

"I'm tired and I think I'm going to bed now," Laura said, getting up from the table.

James hurried after her. He shut the door of her room and leant against it.

"I wish you'd stop needling Julian," he said angrily. "It's stupid pretending we don't know anything about Col Depraz and Paccot. He'll tell Julian what you did as soon as he sees him."

James resented being drawn into a world where motives had to be hidden, questions from people he loved evaded.

"Julian's going to sell Paccot's collar to this man Navier," Laura said woodenly.

"Do you think I care? Why shouldn't Paccot sell it—it's his. The way you're acting you'd think it was yours."

Laura blushed, not from shame but from anger with herself. She still reproached herself for forgetting that Paccot had locked the door. She glanced at the mark on her arm. If only she'd been cleverer. She wondered if Paccot ever left his shed or the col, if there was ever a time when the cat was not alert and watchful.

James pushed himself away from the door and stood close to Laura.

"Why did you try to steal it? I want to know."

Laura looked at her fingers spread out on the bed.

"Didn't you see the pattern on it? It has the same ears of wheat and the same face as the bracelet."

"You mean they're a set."

"Something like that."

"I wonder if it's as spooky as the bracelet," James said lightly not wanting to make Laura so tense and angry she'd tell him nothing, "if Paccot has nightmares."

"Spooky! Oh, James it's not spooky. I know you're worried, but you can't do anything." She looked up at James and suddenly caught hold of his hand, squeezing it so tightly she saw him wince.

"We're seeing Madame Boulard, the day after tomorrow, on Monday, Laura. Can't she help? You saw a murder, don't you realize she thinks you're in danger?"

Reluctantly she let go of James's hand. "I don't trust her anymore."

"The truth is you don't trust anyone—try Madame Boulard. You may have to, whatever you think."

Monday was stiflingly hot. The air in the valley was lifeless and heavy. To the west the mountains crouched threateningly in a suffocating haze which blurred their sharp edges and chiseled cliffs. The heat burned their eyes and their nostrils pricked.

Matthieu was sitting outside his café when Laura and James walked past. He smiled sourly at them and then went back to his columns of figures.

As Laura pushed open Madame Boulard's gate, a lizard toasting itself on the dusty verge of the road flicked into the dead leaves and cobwebs under the privet hedge.

Despite the heat Madame Boulard's garden was cool and lush. A sprinkler twirled on the lawn and they were grateful for the drops which showered them as they walked up the path.

Madame Boulard was sitting under the honeysuckle arbor. She looked as cool as her gray eyes. James wondered why there was a folded map beside her on the seat. They sat down and waited for the first question of their lesson. Madame Boulard stretched her fingers as if she was making up her mind what to say.

"I've thought so much about what happened on Friday," she said quickly. "I was so disturbed I could hardly sleep that night."

Laura kept her eyes on the lawn sprinkler.

"Oh, I'm fine." Laura half-wished she could tell Madame Boulard everything that Loen had learned from Gian, but she couldn't forget her suspicion that Madame Boulard had not told the truth about following them up the mountain. She vaguely heard the back door of the café open. Matthieu was plodding about on the other side of the hedge.

Madame Boulard's next remark made Laura forget Matthieu.

"Do you think Julian really would sell your gold bracelet?"

"I never said it was gold." Laura glared angrily at James.

"Oh, Laura," Madame Boulard said reprovingly. "James hasn't betrayed you. I found out for myself. It wasn't difficult."

To Laura's surprise Madame Boulard unfolded the map and laid it on the grass.

"What's a map to do with it?" Laura was still staring angrily at James.

"Everything. That's your house." She pointed to a spot ringed with red pencil. "All I needed was a pendulum for finding gold."

James remembered what she had said the other day.

"Is it made of gold?" he asked avidly. He saw himself digging up vast hoards which had lain for centuries under innocent-looking tufts of grass.

"No, James. The pendulum is the right length for finding gold."

"What's that?"

"For me, eighteen centimeters."

She took something from the pocket of her simple expensive-looking dress.

"This is what I use."

James expected to see something elaborate, complicated, scientific looking. He was disappointed. The pendulum was just a small wooden ball tied to a string which was wound up on a stick no bigger than a pencil. Madame Boulard unwound the string and leant forward.

"I'll try this forest first."

Madame Boulard held the pendulum over a splash of green on the map. The pendulum did not move.

"There's nothing there."

She held the pendulum threateningly over the red circle marking their house.

"Watch!" she said sharply.

For a moment the pendulum was motionless. Then it started to move remorselessly in slow even circles, around and around and around. Madame Boulard's hand was rock still.

"Let me try that," James implored.

"Not yet."

Laura turned her head. As if purposely breaking the spell of the circling pendulum, Matthieu's cat strolled through the hedge and started cleaning its teeth on one of the poles holding up the arbor.

Madame Boulard pursed her lips angrily. She dropped the pendulum on the map and clapped her hands an inch from the cat's face. It sauntered disdainfully back to Matthieu's. Madame Boulard stood up and faced the hedge.

"Monsieur Matthieu!" she called. "Monsieur Matthieu!"

There was no answer.

"Monsieur Matthieu, please stop your cat coming through my hedge."

James was sorry Madame Boulard denied the cat the splendors of her garden and wanted it confined to Matthieu's barren dusty patch littered with crates of empty wine bottles.

"It's odd but if there's a cat in a house which I'm searching with my pendulum, even if it's only on the map, I can detect nothing."

"We saw an enormous cat on Saturday," James said.

He looked at the map. He put his thumb on the red circle and his little finger on Col Depraz, using his hand as a pair of dividers to measure the distance between the two points. So that was it. The pendulum could find one small bracelet in their house, but Paccot's cat made it miss the soapbox with the collar. He wondered if Madame Boulard knew Paccot had a cat.

"Why is your finger on Col Depraz?" Madame Boulard asked.

"We walked up there the other day," James said distantly. For a moment he wondered if using the pendulum would be as easy as using the copper wire. He wished Matthieu's cat had not interrupted Madame Boulard. "Can I try the pendulum now?"

Madame Boulard dismissed James with one of her quick, friendly smiles and turned to Laura.

"You see, Laura, you never said if your bracelet was made of lead, or copper, or bronze."

"Does it matter?"

"Of course. I was sure a bracelet able to transform you into someone else would be made of a finer metal. I guessed it was gold. I only used the pendulum to amuse myself, to see if my guess was correct."

"Well it is gold," Laura admitted.

"Then you must lend it to me, Laura. You told me you saw a murder. It's not just yourself, we're all involved. Now that you've told me so much, I feel responsible, especially as you think you can't tell Julian or your mother."

James caught Madame Boulard giving Laura a look of such genuine concern he thought she was mad to doubt Madame Boulard's sincerity. *That's just one more crazy idea of Laura's,* he thought, *she must trust Madame Boulard.*

"There's a gold collar as well as a bracelet." James spoke spontaneously, without thinking about the consequences.

Madame Boulard gripped his hand.

"Tell me about it, James."

"I can't—it's all mixed up with Julian."

James couldn't say any more. Paccot had told them to tell no one, even threatened them.

"You must let me have the bracelet, Laura." Madame Boulard pushed her hands distractedly through her hair which fell perfectly into place. "You don't understand how dangerous these experiences can be."

"It's not that at all," Laura said sharply. She resented the implication that she was stupidly perverse. "There's a curse on the bracelet. Letting you borrow it won't help. There's only one way you can."

Madame Boulard's eyes lit up.

"Yes?"

"Go on, Laura, it won't matter," James insisted.

"If you could . . ." Laura stopped. Paccot blocked her way like a wall of steel. Madame Boulard could do nothing—nor could anyone else.

Madame Boulard looked critically at her ankles and slender feet.

"You're being ridiculously obstinate. Let me drive up to your house this afternoon. You could show it to me then."

"I can't, Julian's there."

"Ah, yes, I'd forgotten Julian. I suppose you think I'll sell your bracelet too. Incidentally, I saw him at Col Depraz the other day. I'd gone up to see the view and Julian was coming out of Paccot's shed. Paccot's never even let me see inside."

"Perhaps Paccot's hiding something which he'll only show Julian," Laura said mockingly.

"Perhaps you're right," Madame Boulard said, picking up Laura's joking tone. "Perhaps Paccot has a shed full of golden cheeses he's selling to Julian."

"Why not!"

James felt Laura was deliberately hinting that Paccot did in fact have the collar and that it was the kind of treasure Madame Boulard could hold and hear more than faint conversations and see more than the dim corners of rooms. James wanted to shield Paccot.

"He's only got an old copper cauldron," he said.

"Poor Paccot," Madame Boulard said regretfully. "They're not rich, these mountain farmers. They're all joining cooperatives nowadays and selling their cauldrons to antique dealers. But Julian deals in grander things than copper cauldrons—jewelry for rich collectors, for instance." She paused and then said, "You're taking a great risk, Laura."

Madame Boulard's face was so controlled, so smooth, Laura suddenly realized it was impossible to guess what she was thinking. Behind the calm of gray eyes, the clear skin, the placid brow all kinds of thoughts might be racing; the cruellest calculations might be being made.

She doesn't want to help me, Laura thought suddenly, *she wants to discover what the bracelet will show her. If I lend her the bracelet I might forfeit everything.* Laura let her mind go slack. She knew she had only to wait immobile, withdrawn into herself, and Madame Boulard couldn't touch her.

At last the silence was broken. Madame Boulard sighed and looked at her watch.

"It's time you went home." Madame Boulard's voice was resigned. "We haven't done much work this morning but I have to go out." She looked appraisingly at Laura. "I'd do anything to help you." Her eyes were calculating and determined.

Laura was thankful to hurry down the path. She went out onto the road and waited for James who was helping Madame Boulard open the garage door.

As they passed the corner of Madame Boulard's garden, Laura saw Matthieu. He was standing on the other side of the hedge directly behind the honeysuckle arbor. He was rubbing a bony finger thoughtfully up and down his cheek while the cat swirled around his legs.

13 ‡ *Thunder*

James went into Laura's room to say goodnight to her. She was sitting on her bed looking out of the window. The bracelet lay on her nightdress between her knees.

A fan of heavy black cloud thrust up behind the mountains to the west. At the cloud's edge the sky was a sulphurous blue.

"There's going to be a storm," Laura said without looking at James.

He knelt beside her on the bed. The valley was filling with night. Lights were glinting in houses. The walnut trees shivered in a breeze which came first from one direction, then another.

"I'm worried," James said. Laura stared at the cloud as if she hardly realized James was there.

"What about?" she said at last.

"Do you think Madame Boulard will put two and two together about Paccot's cat?"

Laura's eyes flickered across James's face.

"I don't really care," she said slowly. Her lips were dry and she found it difficult to speak. There was so little time left and so much to do. She let her head fall forward till it rested against the glass. "Oh, James," she said desperately, "I wish I knew how to get that collar."

James looked at the sky. It was covered with black clouds churning above the valley, cutting off the stars.

He could think of no easy answer. He hated the stifling darkness oozing into the room.

"Shall I turn the light on?"

"No. I want to see the storm."

They watched the clouds curdling the sky above the valley. James leaned his cheek against the window frame. The wood was polished by the hands of unknown men and women who during the centuries since the house was built had touched it as they looked out waiting for the snow to thaw in spring or rain to stop in summer.

James and Laura drifted with their thoughts as the approaching storm swallowed up the mountains. The first flash of lightning seared their eyes, leaving a mad vision of blue fields and trees rocking to a furious blast of wind which burst against the house like a wave hitting a sea-wall.

A second flash speared from the cloud, splintering in two glaring rivers hurling themselves into the earth. They waited for the thunder to roll across the sky. It came booming and splintering out of the west to die over their heads and be immediately followed by a second peal. In the silence afterwards they heard a gust of wind rattle the leaves on the walnut trees like a thousand strips of shaken paper.

James counted the seconds between the lightning and the thunder. The storm was still a long way off.

"Should I lend this to Madame Boulard?" Laura said as the bracelet glowed then faded in the lightning. "Do you trust her, James?"

Thunder drummed over the mountains.

"Of course I do."

"It's easy for you," Laura said bitterly.

"All right, if you don't want to lend it her, don't."

James stood up and turned back to look at the bracelet.

"The trouble," he said to it, "is that everyone wants you."

He snatched the bracelet from Laura and held it in front of his face. At that moment lightning flashed.

Jerking around, Laura saw his face hidden by a golden circle leering at her like the eye of a cyclops.

"Give it to me," she yelled through the roar of thunder.

Slowly James lowered the bracelet. He hated Laura's face as it was in the last flash of lightning. His sister looked spectral. She crouched on the bed with both hands stretched out to seize the bracelet. Her lips curled back from her teeth. She was no longer a girl. She was the shadow of a body with a mind rushing away from him to a world filled with malignant phantoms.

He threw the bracelet on the bed. Laura's hands were talons clutching it.

In the silence between peals of thunder his voice was filled with loathing for what he had seen. "Remember what Madame Boulard said might happen to you."

As James shut the door, Laura's fingers slackened their frantic grip on the bracelet. She shook her head violently and deliberately thought about when the rain would fall. Occasionally a few drops cracked like bullets on the eaves above her or spluttered across the grass between the house and the walnut trees.

She rolled on her side and looked through the bracelet. At that moment the window changed to a blinding square blue and chilly with lightning.

The walnut trees vanished. The world was snuffed out like a candle, the lightning quenched.

She was in the forest, blinded by swirling snowflakes, listening to the muffled beat of Loen's horse cantering away over the snow. He had gone with three of his men and left her with Sethor while he searched for Arne and Flear. He daren't take her with him to those dark and terrifying places. Without Loen her heart was like a vast empty space carved out of ice.

Snowflakes tossed and eddied through the trees which grew so close together everything was a lifeless dismal gray. The wind mourning through the trees was pitilessly cold.

She touched the rime of snow sticking to her cloak. Her arm ached. The bracelet was a band of pain which never left her, the collar around her neck a heavy suffocating weight.

She heard footsteps. Sethor was coming toward her leading their horses.

"We must get back before nightfall, Merta."

He gave her the reins and she mounted, wincing from the pain in her arm.

The snow groaned under the horses' hoofs. Sethor rode

beside her. He was humming to himself, occasionally talking to his horse.

She watched the snow fall and stick to her horse's mane. There were three days left before the moon died. That night and the next she would be alone, and then Loen would come back. She wondered if she'd ever again stand in the yard outside Loen's hall listening to the chinking of blackbirds in the dusk and see a thin, new moon hanging low in the western sky.

All of a sudden her horse stopped and snorted, fluttering its nostrils, throwing its head and making the harness jingle.

"Get on." She kicked her heels into the horse's ribs.

"What's got into him?" Sethor said. "Let me ride in front, perhaps he'll follow me."

Sethor rode on, but still her horse wouldn't move. She smacked her hand on its rump.

The horse reared, throwing her back in the saddle. It jerked wildly around and bolted between the trees.

She crouched forward with her face pressed to the horse's mane. She galloped weaving and twisting into the forest. Branches smashed against her, hard dead briars ripped her clothes. Twigs scratched the backs of her hands. Hoofs pounded, the muscles in the shoulders pulsed and flexed. The ears were laid back, the nostrils flared, rimmed with blood.

The horse galloped on and on, never slackening his pace. She let herself flow with the nimble jinking movement of the horse threading a path under the trees whose branches were so thickly matted one into the other that hardly any snow had reached the ground.

She saw a lighter patch in the gloom ahead of her. The

trees were thinning out. There was a tatter of winter sky. Her horse galloped to the edge of a wide, level clearing and just as suddenly as he had bolted, stopped. His legs were quivering and as he tossed his head she could see his eyes rolling with fright.

"Whoa, then," she said stroking the horse's neck to calm it.

The horse grew quieter and Merta looked around the clearing. It was almost a perfect circle cut out of the forest and covered in a deep layer of snow. In the center of the circle grew an enormous pine, the top so high it disappeared in the swirling maze of snowflakes drifting down onto its great sweeping branches of black drooping needles. The tree drew Merta to it, urging her to cross the unmarked snow.

There was not a sound, just absolute stillness and the clean level sheet of snow surrounding the tree. She listened for Sethor's horse riding after her. She caught the faint beat of hoofs. He was riding slowly, not risking his neck in a mad gallop through the trees.

Merta dismounted and tied her horse to a sapling on the edge of the clearing. She walked toward the tree, sinking up to her knees at each step. The snow was so wonderfully smooth and soft and deep.

When she reached the tree she looked back. The snow was falling faster. Her horse was a snowy gray shape. Sethor had just ridden out of the forest.

She started walking around the tree. The lower branches were weighed down to the ground by snow and were so dense she could not even see the trunk. On the far side she found that some of the branches had died. There was a narrow tunnel leading into the trunk which was the color of greeny gray stone. She edged between the branches and found herself under a roof of twigs and snow. It was like standing in a semicircular room. A tongue of snow had drifted through the tunnel, but close to the trunk the ground was dry and covered with dead needles. She put her hand on a drop of resin oozing out of the bark. It was hard like gold.

She heard Sethor calling to her and as she turned to go back to him she saw a lock of black hair caught in one of the branches.

I suppose it's from some animal, she thought, touching it. The hair was soft. It was human hair. Her heart was racing. She looked up.

"Sethor!" she shouted, "Sethor!"

Two shoes ragged and worn into holes pointed down at her upturned face. She saw yellow toenails and cracked, dirt-encrusted skin.

She threw herself into the clearing. Sethor was floundering toward her.

"There's a man hanging there."

Sethor pushed past her. She watched him swing into the tree and heard his knife cutting.

He lowered the body of a man covered in shabby clothes, one of the dead hands caught in a branch. Sethor swore to himself as he struggled with the weight. He lost his grip and a bundle of rags all jutting arms and legs and lolling head tumbled to the ground.

Sethor carried the body out from under the tree and laid it at her feet.

Arne's dead face stared up at her. His eyes were open, the mouth closed, held tight by a rope of plaited straw cutting into his neck. His black hair lay tangled on the snow.

She bent down and touched his cheek. It was hard like wax. She wanted him to forgive her for not understanding him when he was alive.

"Sethor, will Loen ever find Flear and Tural?"

Snow swirled around them, stinging their eyes. Arne's black hair was disappearing under snow. She felt she was already dead like Arne, that soon her cheeks would be as cold and stiff as his, her lips bloodless, her body as insignificant.

"We must take him home, Sethor."

She stood up and helped Sethor carry Arne to their horses. Freezing tears ran down her cheeks.

Thunder rolled up the valley, rumbling from one mountain to the next. The window was a lighter patch set in the utter blackness of the walls. A flurry of wind rattled the walnut leaves and she touched the blanket on her bed.

She tightened her fingers on the bracelet willing it to take her back to Merta, but she could feel time surrounding her like a wall.

Soon her misery and care became a discordant dream.

An hour passed. Lightning split the air above the house, smashing into the fields beyond the walnut trees. Laura woke, her head cracking with thunder. Another bolt jagged down and the crumbling detonation that followed brought the rain. First, great splatting drops—then the earth was laced with water pelting on stones, flattening the grass.

Laura rubbed her eyes and stared through the window at the valley flaring in the lightning. The walnut trees swayed and twisted in the wind. The ground was prickly with stripped leaves and torn branches. Laura slipped the bracelet on her arm and hugged her knees to her chin. Her eyes ached from the brilliant white of lightning and the intense darkness. The rain was like a waterfall pouring from the roof and sluicing down the path beside the house.

A lightning bolt struck the forest on the other side of the valley and a tree roared into a sheet of yellow flame and then died to an ember, like a match shaken out in a darkened room.

She waited for the storm to end, but it was trapped in the valley unable to fight its way over the crest of mountains to the east. The thunder was almost continuous, sometimes cracking like guns, at others bellowing through the clouds.

Lightning bloomed over the meadows and Laura's heart jumped.

There was someone out there!—a blue-white figure in the storm peering at the house. She shut her eyes to drive away what she had seen. Someone was standing under the walnut trees waiting to be hidden by darkness.

She edged back from the window dreading the next flash. When it came there was no one there. She lay back in the dark, her ears stretched for the slightest sound.

Outside the walls of her bedroom pebbles ground together. Someone was coming up the path beside the house. There was a tap against the wall. In the blackness of her room, Laura heard the rustling scrape of stiff, heavy clothes. A shoe sucked out of mud. Laura held her breath. Suddenly the window rattled, then stopped. The catch

jarred as the window shook again. Laura was unable to cry
out, unable to make the one stride to the door and save
herself by slamming it shut against whoever was testing
the window. Fingertips squeaked over the glass as lightning ricocheted into the room.

She saw an open hand dripping with rain, and a face.
Two eyes glared at her from black sockets in a white head.
Nothing else, just a hand and a head fired by lightning.

Laura's mouth broke open in a scream which was buried
in a tumbling mountain of thunder. The window smashed
open, crashing back against the wall. A cataract of rain
poured into her face. A cold wet hand brushed her shoulder. She was deafened by the downpour and the continuous
roll of thunder. The hand touched her again and searching
fingers ran over her skin.

She tried to hurl herself off the bed and escape but the
hand gripped her above the elbow wrenching her toward
the window. She fought in the darkness, twisting like a
snake. She couldn't break the grip which pressed her muscles tight to the bone. She bent her head around and bit
the fingers holding her. They were hard on her lips. Her
head was pulled away by the hair and her arm was bent
behind her back and forced upward. Fingers slithered over
her shoulder. She felt her arm was going to break. Her
breath came in great sobs of pain. She flailed her free hand
to scratch the terrible white face she had seen in the lightning and touched a cold, smooth forehead wet with rain,
eyebrows, flickering lashes. She snatched her hand away.
The face felt dead it was so cold.

Suddenly the bracelet tugged against her arm, was
dragged over her wrist, puckering up her skin. It was
forced over her hand. For a second she caught it, but her

fingers were torn open and she was thrown to the floor.

Lightning burned outside the window. Nobody was there. The casement swung idly in a gust of wind.

Laura screamed, her voice rising high and desperate through the thunder. She screamed at the open window glaring in the lightning and the threat of a white face gazing at her. She lay on the floor too weak with fear to move and cried for the stolen bracelet and for safety from the real terror of thunder and lightning and figures under the trees. She cried and touched her arm. It was wet with rain.

Laura's screams woke James. He rushed into her room never expecting to find Julian kneeling beside her.

Laura was huddled on the floor and her hair was wet and hung bedraggled around her face. A trickle of blood was running down her chin from a cut on her lip.

"Laura, don't cry." Julian put his arms around her. "What happened, Laura?"

"I will never see Loen again," was all she said, over and over.

"What do you mean?"

A sudden flurry of wind blew the curtains; rain poured into the room.

"Shut the window, James. I thought you fixed that catch." Julian did not look at James. "Who came in?" he asked Laura.

"He came from under the walnut trees."

"What's she talking about?" Julian turned to James.

James wondered how he could explain things to Julian which he didn't understand himself.

"I suppose the storm blew the window open," he said hesitantly.

"It wasn't the wind. He took it." Laura twisted her head around to face James. "It's gone."

Julian suddenly picked Laura up and carried her into the living room and put her down in an armchair.

"Get a blanket from your bed, James, and tell your mother to come down."

When James came running back with the blanket, Julian was holding a glass to Laura's mouth.

"Take the glass," he said, snatching the blanket from James and tucking it around Laura. "You have a nip too, it's brandy."

Julian caught hold of Laura's arm.

"What's that?" he almost shouted.

The tanned skin bore livid marks made by vicious bruising fingers.

"He held me there." Laura rested her head on the back of the chair.

"Who?"

Thunder rolled over the mountains to the east. The storm was at last breaking over the peaks to spit out its rage in snow and ice.

Laura looked weakly at James. "He's taken it back," she said.

"What are you talking about, Laura?" Julian sat on the arm of the chair. He was trying to massage away the marks on Laura's skin when her mother came down the stairs.

"Laura, darling, what's the matter?" She anxiously kissed Laura's forehead. "Did you roll out of bed? You've even cut your lip."

"Look at that." Julian pointed at Laura's arm.

Their mother flinched. She glanced swiftly, fearfully at Julian. "What's happened? Why didn't you wake me earlier?"

Laura swung her head from side to side to shake away the eyes which she could still see staring at her from the heart of the storm. They were so envious, so madly determined.

"He stole it," she said again.

"Laura!" Julian's voice was hard, urgent. "What do you mean, what was stolen?"

"Her bracelet," James said.

"What bracelet?" Julian asked quickly. "Is that what you were on about the other day?"

"She found it in the river. It was gold."

Laura looked away from the three faces peering down at her. They were remote and uninteresting. She wanted to be with Loen and know that he had killed Flear and Tural.

"Why didn't you tell us about it?" her mother asked.

Laura knew she had to speak. There was no longer a need for secrecy.

"It was what Julian said when I came back from fishing that morning."

Julian stood up and threw a log on the dying fire.

Her mother said, "Do you mean you've been brooding about that for days?"

Far away they could hear the thunder, but the rain had stopped and around the house the night was still.

"Why did Julian search my room?"

"Search your room!" Julian said exasperatedly.

"Please, Julian," their mother said. "Wasn't that the morning we went into Annecy to meet Navier?" She paused. "The morning I found all your wet clothes on the floor, Laura. I looked in your chest of drawers to see if you had any clean ones left."

Laura touched the cut on her lip. She glanced at Julian. He was the same man who had shouted at her.

"I still want to know who broke into your room," Julian said.

"Could it be . . ." Laura stopped herself. She was going to say "Tural." She remembered the roar of wind as the window cracked open, the feel of cold, strong fingers freezing around her arm, the deadness of the flesh. The marks on her were like the stigma of a predatory animal, the puncturing teeth, the ripping claws. "I don't know, I don't know."

"Don't worry, we'll find out," Julian said determinedly. "You must try to go to sleep."

"I'll see you to bed," their mother said. "Come on, James."

James followed his mother and Laura. He shut his door after he said goodnight and lay in bed thinking about Julian.

Laura looked at her arm. The strange white mark had vanished. There were only the savage bruises made by a rain-drenched hand. She thought of the empty hiding place James had made. Without the bracelet she was banished from Merta's time forever. She almost regretted her new-found safety. *I'll never be with Loen again,* she thought, *or hear the rush of hoofs, or know if Merta lived.* She wanted the weak comfort of tears.

She switched off the light.

Instinctively she looked out of the window at the walnut trees. Above them the stars were shining in a clear sky. A gentle wind rustled the leaves. The night was calm—so calm she could just hear the yowling of a cat coming from so far away she was not sure how long ago the cat had cried.

14 ‡ Hand in the Water

James lay in bed with his hands behind his head and stared at the wooden ceiling which was glowing a deep honey brown in the morning sunlight.

Poor Laura, he thought, *she used to hate thunderstorms. She should have told Julian about the bracelet from the beginning. He'll chew me into little bits when he finds the hole I made in the wall.*

James looked idly at the window and wondered where the bracelet could be now. The window was half-open and the curtains swung slowly backward and forward in the breeze.

"Got it!" James said exultantly. "Why didn't I think of that before."

He scrambled into his clothes and pushed his feet into

run-down rope-soled shoes. *I won't go through the house,* he thought, remembering Julian's attack on Laura, *I'll wake everyone up.* He climbed through the window and ran soundlessly up to the barn.

James opened an old gimcrack wardrobe where Julian stored paints and brushes and dented biscuit tins heavy with rusty nails and priceless broken screws which might be useful someday. In a jam jar he found a wooden ball which had once been tied to the end of a rope used to start a lawn mower. The ball was scratched and rough and still bore traces of red paint. It was exactly what James needed to make a pendulum. He put the ball in his pocket and ran back to his bedroom window and climbed through.

There was a pencil on the table and a piece of string in his jacket pocket. He unravelled about a meter of string, tied one end to the pencil, threaded the other through the hole in the ball and tied another knot.

Eighteen centimeters. He remembered the number clearly. Madame Boulard had been quite definite. Eighteen centimeters.

He measured the string between the ball and the pencil. All at once he was filled with doubt, unable to decide if Madame Boulard meant the length of the string or the length of the whole pendulum. His hands dithered as he tried to make up his mind. "I'll make it the length of the string," he said under his breath, feeling less and less confident that he could make the pendulum work. He wound string around the pencil till there were exactly eighteen centimeters between the pencil and the wooden ball.

James took the map on which he had found Col Depraz and spread it out on the table. Many of the folds were torn, leaving frayed gaps in the countryside.

Almost reluctantly James picked up the pencil and moved his hand till the wooden ball hung above the black square marking his house on the map. I know there's gold here, he said to himself, there's Mum's wedding ring and Julian's gold watch.

But the pendulum did not move. The wooden ball was obstinately still.

James's hand wobbled. He suddenly realized that practically every black spot on the map marked a house. There were thousands of houses and in them hands with gold rings opening cupboards, writing letters, sweeping floors, shaving faces. *If I get the pendulum to work,* James thought, *how do I know I haven't found a pair of gold spectacles or a mouth full of gold fillings?* He saw rows of tumblers holding false teeth with gold hooked pieces to anchor them firmly onto stumps in naked gums.

He stared glumly at the map spotty with houses. His eyes traced the river through the white meadows in the valley into the dark green forest, where he and Laura had met Madame Boulard, and onto the bare, pale green, treeless mountains.

Then he remembered Paccot's soapbox with the gold collar.

He steadied the wooden ball over the black spot on the summit of Col Depraz. The pendulum refused to move.

"I know there's gold there," James reassured himself. His arm was beginning to cramp. The pendulum was so lifeless it might have been made of lead.

He wondered if he had measured the length of string correctly.

"I'll make it a bit longer," he said, twisting the pencil.

Still nothing happened.

"Perhaps it's the cat. Perhaps it has the same affect on me as it would on Madame Boulard. I'll try a bit more."

A tremor passed into his hand. The pendulum started to move slowly in a circle, around and around it swung, purposefully sensing the gold hidden in the cardboard box.

James held his breath as the pendulum gained momentum. His lungs were bursting before he dared let them collapse and gasp in air again.

There was no doubt. His hand holding the pencil was firm. He knew he was not cheating. Gold had made the pendulum move in its probing circle.

"I can do it!" He let his hand fall on the map. The wooden ball rolled stupidly across the paper.

James looked at the area he had to search. It was enormous. *I suppose I'll have to start somewhere,* he thought.

He straightened out the string and held the pendulum above his house and moved his hand so that the pendulum traced an ever-widening spiral. He searched slowly, not knowing how long he had to hover over one place before the pendulum could sense what lay there and start its own circling movement.

On the fourth twist of the spiral his hand tingled. He held it still; the pendulum began to circle.

James stared at the map. The wooden ball was over two dots on the edge of the village. His arm ached with the effort of holding his hand motionless and of resisting the force working through the pendulum.

If he was to believe Madame Boulard, somewhere in that group of houses lay a piece of gold bigger than a filling or a wedding ring.

He let the pendulum fall and looked at the dots which had started the pendulum circling. His finger stabbed the map. One of those dots was the house with the honey-suckle arbor.

God, he thought, *perhaps Laura's right after all.*

Shall I tell Laura? James asked himself. It was almost mid-day and he was still unable to make up his mind.

He couldn't believe the pendulum had told the truth. After all, Laura was so insistent it was a man who had stolen the bracelet—how could it possibly be Madame Boulard?

James picked a scale of blistered paint off the barn door. *If I tell Laura she'll belt off to the village and start accusing Madame Boulard, it'll be worse than Paccot's shed.* He knew if he tried to go down there by himself to use the pendulum closer to Madame Boulard's house, Laura would think he was plotting some enormous treachery and follow him.

He looked down the hillside. Laura and his mother were under the walnut trees.

I could tell Julian. James turned the idea over in his mind. Reluctantly he decided he'd have to risk Julian's scorn. There was no other way.

He walked slowly down to the walnut trees. Laura was lying with her hands under her head and their mother was doing a crossword.

"Where's Julian?" James asked.

"He's trying to catch some trout for lunch." His mother wrote in the answer to a clue. Her hand moved quickly, jabbing the ball-point into the paper.

Laura opened her eyes and said softly, "James, where do you think the bracelet is now?"

Their mother dropped the paper on her knee and pushed her sunglasses up on top of her head.

"I don't want to hear any more about that bracelet. It makes me sick thinking of what might have happened to you last night, Laura. Now both of you go and find Julian. Tell him I'm hungry. If he's caught nothing we'll have an omelette."

Laura jumped up abruptly and strode away from her mother. James followed her.

The meadows were beaten flat by the rain and in places the ground was boggy, squelching underfoot. Their feet were soaking wet when they reached the wood which had become a wilderness of torn branches. Sodden leaves covered the ground and the moss on the stones was greasy. As they threaded their way to the pool where Julian liked to fish, the bushes sprayed them with a thousand drops of water at the slightest touch.

The river had risen after the storm and was thick and brown and killed all sounds with its endless rush. Laura pitched a stone into the middle and saw the current whip the splash downstream.

There was no sign of Julian.

"I've never seen it run so fast," James shouted in Laura's ear. "What shall we do? We can't call Julian, the water makes too much noise."

Laura peered up and down stream for a rod held low over the water.

"Let's go upstream." She stood for a moment and, as if she'd remembered a long-forgotten habit, searched the water for a fish.

Julian could not be far. They walked slowly along the bank under the trees expecting to see him at any moment. At last they came to the spot where Laura had found the bracelet. The rock on which she had stood holding it for the first time was submerged. The river raced over it, breaking in a curling eddy of whitish brown water. In the sunlight glancing through the leaves Laura felt a door had slammed in her face and that she would never be able to open it again.

They walked on, their ears ringing with the sound of water. Just before they reached the boulders blocking the head of the pool, Laura turned back to see the rock once more, but it was lost in the hurrying river.

Then Laura looked up the boulder looming over her. From it hung an arm. Water spouted from the finger tips.

"James!" she shouted, "James!"

The fingers were moving with the flurry of water pouring over them. Laura wanted to run away. On the other side of the boulder lay a dead man, drowned, his lungs full of water. She was sure of it! His cold wet lips would touch hers as she tried to breathe life into his body. Her hands were clammy as she forced herself to the top of the fall.

Julian was lying on his stomach, with his face out of the water. A trickle of blood had run over his cheek from a deep cut on the side of his head. His face was white as chalk and his eyes were shut. His right hand held a loop of string threaded through the gills of four trout.

She clutched James's arm and shouted, "Go and get help, James. I'll wait here, hurry."

She saw him slide down the boulder and run zigzagging through the wood, leaping over brambles, charging through bushes.

Laura knelt beside Julian and took the string out of his hand, then held his wrist to let her fingers press between bone and sinew to find if he was alive. She sensed the faint beating of his heart.

She daren't try and turn him onto his back. She dreaded the wound on his head hitting the rock. He was too heavy to move into the shelter of the trees. She took his hand from the water and laid it at his side.

She watched the scab thicken and grow dark on Julian's head and wondered how long he had been lying there before they had found him.

She sat back on her heels and felt useless. She had to wait for someone to come. She looked intently at Julian to see if there were any injuries which she had not noticed before. There was a gap between Julian's trousers and his socks, showing white skin matted with black hair.

Two flies were hovering over the wound on Julian's head. One fly landed on the wound and started walking on its stiff needle legs. Laura brushed it away. She held Julian's hand. *He must know there's someone here,* she thought.

Laura was trapped by sorrow, remorse, fear for Julian's life. She wanted to be honest with herself and not feel emotions which were not truly hers. She knew she had been unjust, but hadn't he been equally unjust? She could not love Julian simply because her mother had married him. But she could be fair to him.

Laura searched Julian's face. His flesh clung to the bone making him look old and drawn. She needed months, years even, to know him and then—perhaps—then knowledge might turn to love. There was no other way. She waited longing to hear the sound of her mother or James coming with help. Julian was so pale, every now and again his lips trembled. His hand was so cold in hers. She wished she could tell him what she felt.

At last she heard her mother's frantic voice cutting through the roar of water falling into the pool. Laura stood up and waved. James was already clambering up the boulder followed by men carrying a stretcher.

Her mother crouched beside Julian. Her fingers fluttered over his body.

Laura and James watched Julian being turned over onto his back, being lifted onto the stretcher, being carried laboriously through the wood. All the time their mother hovered close to Julian, touching him, telling the men to be careful.

The ambulance had been driven down the meadow and was waiting on the other side of the trees.

Just as the stretcher was about to be lifted in, Julian regained consciousness. His lips moved as if he was trying to speak. He managed to lift his hand and beckon James and Laura.

They leaned over him.

"Warn Paccot," Julian whispered, "warn Paccot."

"What about?" James asked desperately.

Julian waved his hand and looked imploringly at him, "Warn Paccot."

James' mother came fussing back. She'd been arguing with the driver.

"James! Laura! Don't try and make him talk." She looked distractedly from the stretcher to the ambulance. "I'll have to stay with him in the hospital tonight, I can't leave him. They've agreed to give me a lift. You'll have to look after yourselves. If there's anything you want, telephone Madame Boulard."

James and Laura watched their mother climb into the ambulance. Two Red Cross flags fluttered from its roof as it drove bumping and swaying up the meadow.

15 ‡ *Burning*

"We must go to Col Depraz at once," Laura said urgently.

James looked intently at her. "Do you think Julian fell?"

"I hated seeing him like that, there was nothing I could do." She listened to the faint wailing of the ambulance swooping down the hill to the village. "Someone might have attacked him."

"Come on," James said. "Maybe you're right. We have to hurry."

As they neared the river, Laura shivered. The wind was blowing sharp and cold from the northwest. The sky was a clean blue without a cloud.

While he pelted up the path through the forest, James wondered what Paccot would do when they gave him Julian's warning. *Probably drive us off the col before we can tell him,* he thought despondently.

"James," Laura said as they passed out of the forest, "perhaps the person who attacked Julian stole my bracelet."

They stopped to rest for a minute on a smooth rock rising over a sea of wind-blown grass and flowers. The wind was flowing up the mountain like water, flattening the grass in rippling swathes. The sky was covering with a milky film of thickening cloud.

"You're certain it was a man?" James asked.

Laura nodded.

But the pendulum, James thought, *circled Madame Boulard's house.*

"I'm cold," Laura said, "let's get on, the weather's changing."

She jumped off the rock and began the climb over the vast expanse of grass lapping the mountain to the summit of the col.

They crossed the stream with the wind tearing at their clothes and whipping their hair around their cheeks. At last they stood looking down on the roof of Paccot's shed.

The ground was now a mass of puddles. For an instant the wind dropped and they heard the dull clonking of bells. From the other side of the col a cow heaved itself onto the muddy ground beside the shed and was followed by the rest of the herd.

Then they saw Paccot. He was leading a string of goats down the slope of the mountain to the west. He came striding over the cropped grass swinging a long thin stick. When he saw them he waved it threateningly in the air.

James and Laura slithered down the bank and took

shelter in the lee of the shed. They waited for Paccot with their backs pressed tight to the wall. The wind screeched over their heads.

Paccot drove the goats up to the shed. Their udders wagged between their legs like socks filled with sand.

"Why have you come back here?" Paccot growled when he reached them. "I don't want you near this place."

"Julian told us to," Laura said defiantly. "He's hurt."

Paccot glowered distrustfully at her.

"We found him by the river," James said. "He was unconscious. Just before he was taken away in the ambulance he told us to warn you."

"Warn me of what?"

"He couldn't say, he's very ill."

"Why should I believe you, or you?" Paccot swung around and stabbed a finger at Laura's face.

"Someone stole Laura's bracelet last night," James said, as if that explained everything.

"What bracelet?" Paccot looked fiercely at Laura.

"When I was fishing one day I found a gold bracelet in the river. Someone broke into the house and took it from me."

"Will your stepfather be home tonight? He wanted to see me."

"He can't see you, his head's all cut."

Paccot drove the point of his stick into the ground.

"I suppose you told half the village what I keep up here?"

"Of course we didn't." Laura felt gooseflesh crawling up her back. "Julian must have meant that whoever stole my bracelet might try and steal your collar."

"Why should they? Nobody knows anything about it. Unless you've told them. Your stepfather wouldn't."

Paccot turned and looked at his cows and goats waiting to be milked as if there was nothing more to be said.

"I suppose we should go home now." James looked unhappily at Laura. He dreaded the long walk down into the valley back to an empty house with no one to welcome them.

Paccot looked at the sky and said, "You're not going anywhere."

While they had been on the col the clouds had sunk lower and lower. The mountains had disappeared and above the col only a narrow band of light separated the wind-blown grass from the surging clouds. As they watched, the band of light vanished. Traces of fog blew around them.

"We'll get home if we hurry," Laura said defiantly, treating Paccot's warning as she had Julian's.

Paccot gripped Laura's arm.

"You're not leaving here," he said sternly. "Not when there's a fog." He didn't try to reason with her as Julian might.

"We know the way."

"You're not leaving, though you deserve to be thrown out." He jerked his thumb in the direction of his shed. "Tonight you sleep in the loft."

Laura said, "I know what you must think of me, but we didn't tell anyone about the gold collar."

Paccot sniffed loudly and looked at the fog seeping down the mountain. "You help me with the milking." He pointed his stick at Laura.

Paccot fetched two plastic buckets and a stool and sat with his head buried in the flank of the first cow. They watched the milk spurting into the bucket. The cow chewed the cud and twitched its ears. At last Paccot gave it a smack on the rump and it lumbered off into the fog, its bell ringing. Laura and James carried the full buckets of milk to the shed and emptied them into the cauldron.

After he had milked the cows Paccot came into the shed where Laura had just emptied the last bucket. He kicked the embers under the cauldron and then reached down lengths of pinewood and laid them on the fire.

"You make some beds," he said to James. "Climb up there."

He showed James a ladder fixed to the wall and gave him a gas lantern, the kind campers use.

"Come and help milk the goats," he said to Laura. "I want you where I can keep an eye on you."

James waited till Paccot and Laura left the shed and then lit the lantern. He climbed the ladder and had to stoop when he stepped into the loft.

What does Paccot expect me to do, he said to himself as he looked around. He could see only a collection of old cans, a long row of empty wine bottles, and in one corner a lump which looked like the carcass of an animal. James approached it warily. It was a pile of goatskins.

He put the lantern on the floor and picked up one of the skins. It was soft and supple and the hair was silky, reminding him of his wineskin. He remembered seeing goatskins for sale on a stall beside the road to Annecy. I suppose this was an unwanted billy, he said to himself. He sniffed the skin. It smelt interestingly of goat.

James cleared a space amongst the cans and made two

goatskin mattresses. He lay down on one to try it for size and thickness. He could only just feel the boards.

He divided the remaining skins evenly so they could use them as covers. Suddenly he heard the cat meowing and realized they would be sleeping right over Paccot's treasure. *I wonder what Laura'll say about that,* he thought, as he climbed down the ladder. He turned out the lantern and went out of the shed.

He could see nothing.

White fog crept around him. It was green where it touched the grass. Paccot and Laura had vanished. He walked a few steps from the door. There were no voices to guide him, no sound of milk squirting into a bucket. Then the fog cleared a little. He turned around. He was thankful to see the door of the shed.

"I'm going back there," he said. "They can find me."

He stood in the doorway watching the fog billow toward him, then retreat. It was deceiving and elusive, hiding everything, masking the brink of cliffs, dulling sounds. Julian was right. Only a fool would go charging about a mountain in this weather.

"Laura!" he called, "Where are you?"

He heard a goat bleating and then the ringing of a bell. The cows were moving farther away.

"Laura, I'm here." *Where else would I be,* he thought, annoyed with himself for calling out something so silly.

Then he heard boots crushing into mud. Paccot and Laura loomed through the fog.

"What's the matter?" Laura said as she followed him into the shed.

"I thought you were lost."

"Shut the door," Paccot ordered, "and keep the filthy

muck out." He went into the room where he stored his cheese.

"Did he say anything?" James asked as he shut the door.

"Only that nobody can come here in this weather."

"Do you think he'll give us anything to eat? I'm starving."

Paccot came back and banged a large loaf and a cheese on the table.

"Come and get the mugs," he told Laura, "while I make coffee."

She followed Paccot hesitantly into the store. When he had shown her the collar she had not noticed a small cookstove and a gas cylinder.

Behind her was the crate. She could hear the cat purring. She looked over her shoulder at it.

"I know what you're thinking," Paccot said scornfully. "Take these and get back to your brother."

He pushed three aluminum mugs into her hand.

James was examining the cheese. It was one of Paccot's more mature examples of his art. Aunt Lydia would have hurled it into the garbage can and then spent an hour or two sterilizing her kitchen. The cheese was covered in green mold.

Paccot cut wedges of cheese and bread. "Eat up," he said.

James filled his mouth with bread and then cautiously bit the tip off the cheese. He expected it to be horrid like stale biscuits, but it was delicious, tasting the way mushrooms smell before they are cooked.

They finished their meal with boiling hot mugs of strong black coffee.

It was getting dark. The fog floated outside the window, baffled by the glass. The room was by now so dusky they could hardly see one another except when a flame leapt up from the fire.

"Go to bed," Paccot said. "I'll light the lantern. You'll be able to see what you're doing if I keep it down here."

Laura followed James up the ladder. In the dim light shining from below she examined the bed James had made for her.

"I'm not going to undress," she said firmly.

"Not even your shoes?"

"No. There might be rats. They're not biting my toes."

James looked quickly around the loft. He dreaded a pair of beady eyes peering at him from a corner and the sound of feet scurrying across the floor.

"Paccot must drink a lot of wine," Laura said as she silently counted the empty bottles.

"He's sober enough. I expect he doesn't bother to take the empties home."

James covered himself with skins and rolled a couple into a hard, furry pillow. He lay back and sighed contentedly.

"I feel like Ghenghis Khan," he said. "He always sleeps on furs in movies."

He stretched out his legs and arms and let his joints go loose. The skins were beautifully warm.

"I'm tired," he whispered. Instantly he fell asleep.

Laura lay with her hands clasped behind her head. *Even if I had the collar,* she thought sorrowfully, *I couldn't do anything without the bracelet. How odd, Julian's given me a second chance to get the collar but it's come too late.* She heard

Paccot moving about and felt the skins stir as James rolled over onto his side. Later Paccot turned out the light and Laura looked up into the blackness of the roof.

She remembered the sound of Loen's horse moving away through the forest. She stared into the dark, while below her the gold collar worked to the echo of Flear's song.

Laura felt the cold against her arms first. She pulled them under the skins. *It must be colder up here in the mountains,* she thought. She started to shiver uncontrollably. She tucked her knees up to her chest and tried to cocoon herself into the goatskins.

The cold crept toward her, trickled along her spine, slithered around her legs. Instinctively she snuggled toward James. She couldn't feel him. Desperately Laura rolled over and forgetting the cold put out a hand to touch James's shoulder. He was not there. Frost stung her nostrils.

Merta's drowsy thoughts slid over Laura like a pane of black glass. She wanted to feel the sun warming her as she walked through cornfields women cut with sickles. The time between the old and the new moon lay before her like a pit spiked with stakes. All that day she'd waited for Loen to come riding up to the hall with two heads hanging from his saddle.

At dawn she'd watched Sethor hack Arne's grave out of the frozen ground. Not knowing his people's customs she did what her people did and put a black jar of grain between Arne's hands. Soon someone might be filling a jar with grain for her journey into death and putting her ivory combs and amber necklace in a grave beside her body. Her ears still ached with the dull sound of a mattock cutting frozen clods to make a grave. For the rest of the day she'd waited for Loen and when at dusk she gave up hope of seeing him come home she tried to resign herself to death. But she couldn't die now without seeing her unborn children or knowing what age was like without Loen to help her through the door.

Wearily she rolled over, shivering despite the weight of the bearskin rug covering her. Her teeth chattered. No one else was awake and the fire in the center of the hall had sunk to a faint red glow in the darkness. It was the time when the world hangs between darkness and light. Outside, the forest was still, held by bitter cold pressing on the branches and flattening the grass under rime.

Then, far away, she heard horses, a faint drumming in the distance. She sat up, pulling the bearskin around her shoulders. Her mouth was dry as sawdust. The hoofs rang on iron-hard ground.

It's Loen coming back! In a few moments I'll know if I'm going to live.

She listened, her body tense with the agony of waiting. He must be passing the hollow oak tree where the owls nest. What will he tell me?

But the hoofbeats stopped so abruptly the horses might have vanished without even an echo to remind her they had been there. She pushed the rug away. The cold bit into her, striking the collar more tightly around her neck.

She heard nothing, not even the embers stirring in the dying fire.

She stood up and ran barefoot to the door. She slid back the bolts and pulled the door open. She took one step outside and stopped.

Torches flared on the other side of the yard. Two hooded men were running toward the barns. They carried blazing torches and drawn swords.

Loen had not come home. It was a burning and she would die.

She heard a voice high-pitched and sweet. Fire seethed up the thatch on the barns and light flowed over Tural standing in the yard, his face pale even in the storm of flames glinting on the twisted patterns hammered into his sword. Horses screamed in the burning stables.

She fled back into the hall. Her eyes were smarting with smoke. There was no time to slide the heavy bolts. Tural had seen her. He was yelling to his men. His voice cut through the roar of flames. In a moment he would be standing over her.

She ran blindly through the hall to the only place where she could hide. There was a low door screened by the pile of logs kept for the fire. Beyond the door was a little room where wine was stored. She slipped behind the logs just as Tural burst into the hall.

I mustn't make a sound. I must be quiet. She crept through the door. Her hands were trembling as she pushed it shut.

She crouched on the floor. There were other men beside Tural in the hall.

"Merta! Merta!" Sethor was calling her.

She couldn't answer him.

She heard Tural's snickering laugh.

"Merta . . ." Sethor's cry died.

"They can't help you, Merta." Tural's voice teased.

Light from torches flickering through a chink moved wildly from side to side, crossing her face like a blade.

I must keep still.

She touched one of the wine jars. The clay was smooth and cool.

"Here! Here!" Tural was a wolf baying.

The logs were bouncing and rolling across the hall. The light grew brighter.

Tural spoke one sweet honeyed word. He had seen the door.

She pressed back against the wall. Her mind rocked with the cracking of fire and smash of falling beams. Her stomach was wet with fear.

"Loen! Loen!" She kept on calling him.

The door ripped open. Tural was a rushing black shape. His fingers were driving the golden collar into her neck and she retched at the sudden stench of smoke clinging to him like his own shroud.

He was pulling her through the door. She clutched one of the wine jars. It rocked, toppled over, splintering against others and wine gushed over the floor which glistened with pools of fire.

Tural's fingers were like vermin on her skin as he dragged her out from the blazing ruin of Loen's hall. He jabbed his sword into the scabbard and gripped her arm above the bracelet.

The sky flowed with sparks and smoke. Horses whinnied and stamped.

She tried to twist her head to see her home for the last time. Instead she saw Sethor lying torn and broken on the snow as Tural wrenched her around. Then Tural was throwing her onto a horse. Rope tugged her wrists, flayed her ankles as they tied her to the saddle.

Tural was dragging the horse forward into darkness pulsing with light from the flames.

He was leading her away into the forest. At the oak tree
he stopped. The snow glimmered with fire and under the
oak tree Merta saw a horse and rider almost merging into
the deep blackness of the trunk. The horse moved slowly
out from the darkness under the branches to the unnatural
fiery snow.

Flear was staring at her. She was so close Merta felt
Flear's breath on her face. Soft fingers touched her cheek.

"I couldn't leave you," Flear whispered. "Loen won't see
you gutter like a candle, but Tural and I will."

Flear wheeled her horse and rode to Tural. Merta heard
Flear kissing her son, saw her embrace him, hold him
close, stroke his long pale hair.

"We must ride fast." Flear's voice was urgent.

Tural dragged Merta's horse forward and then they were
galloping between the trees with Flear's song pouring over
her, piercing its way into her brain.

They had almost reached the river when Tural reined up
and looked back. He pulled her horse around so she could
see the flames lighting up the sky. Then he whipped her
horse on in the last furious gallop to the river bank.

They splashed through the ford, the water burning her
feet with its cold, and up into the gap where she had first
seen Tural leading Arne tied to a horse just as she was
tied.

The horses slowed as they followed the track up the
mountain. As the slope steepened the horses plugged their
way forward, their hoofs slipping on hard ice hidden under
snow.

Tural cursed his horse to move faster. Her own horse's
head was continually savaged and wrenched as Tural pulled
the rope tied to its bridle. Merta could hardly keep

upright in the saddle. Her whole body was aching. She felt encased by an icy shell of fear and hopelessness. Loen could not save her. She would die with Flear's eyes fixed on hers.

Her horse stopped abruptly. Tural was peering ahead in the darkness. A horse and rider blocked the path.

James's lungs were filled with smoke. He sat up, his chest torn with a rasping cough. His mouth tasted of fire. The loft glowed with an angry red light. Flames clutched the rafters behind the row of bottles.

"Laura!" he shouted, "Laura!"

Through the murk of smoke he could see the pile of skins beside him.

"Laura! Where are you?"

He threw the skins aside.

"Paccot! Laura!"

Then he saw her. A thin gray shape lying on the skins. He could see goat hairs in the outline of the head, a floor board through a thrust out hand. She was insubstantial, a ghost.

"She's dead," James cried. Madame Boulard's warning rushed through his mind.

"Hurry!" Paccot shouted. "Wake your sister"

"She's . . ." but James couldn't speak. He looked back at the pile of skins. The ghostly, empty shape of Laura was still lying there.

Paccot was pulling at his ankle, shouting at him to come down. James looked back once more. The transparent hand stretched out on the boards was moving, thickening, becoming flesh. Laura was lying on the goatskins.

James wrenched away from Paccot. He threw himself at Laura and dragged her to the edge of the loft.

Light from the fire glowed and shifted, flashing white and dark, red green. A band of smoke hovered over them pulsing with the heat.

"Quickly!" Paccot poked his head into the loft and grabbed Laura, pulling her down into his arms.

Laura felt the heat searing her as Paccot ran through the burning doorway. She could smell burning hair. Paccot dropped her to the ground.

She sank into the grass still feeling the grip of Tural's hand.

Paccot came back with James in his arms.

"Look at the roof!" Paccot wiped his forehead with his sleeve.

Smoke billowed under the eaves and where the fire was hottest the corrugated iron was glowing red. The empty bottles were exploding like firecrackers.

James stood between Paccot and Laura. His lungs were parched with smoke.

"How did the fire start?" he asked. "Is the cat safe?"

"She's there," Paccot said.

The cat was frantically rubbing its eyes with its fore-paws.

"How did it start?" James asked again.

"Didn't you hear?"

"No." James was shivering despite the heat from the fire.

"The cat woke me. As I lit the lantern someone rushed out and knocked it over. I went after him, but the lantern set the shed alight." Paccot was silent, then he said. "Whoever it was took the collar. He threw pepper in the cat's face."

Without any warning he seized their hands and pulled them away from the fire.

"The gas!" he shouted, "I forgot the gas!"

James looked over his shoulder as he stumbled away from the shed. He was just in time to see the gas cylinder explode. The corrugated iron roof rose up like blown leaves and then fell. The air rocked around them with the force of the explosion and the wailing cat scampered away into the safety of the darkness. The fire burnt within the walls of the shed as if it were in a huge grate, the flames crackling in the same cheerful way they crackle on a hearth. The air reeked with the stench of burning skins.

"Who did it?" Laura asked.

Paccot shook his head. "I've nothing left." He coughed and spat into the grass.

In the light from the fire James saw a piece of string tied to a wooden ball lying at his feet.

He snatched it up.

"It's the pendulum," he shouted. "Madame Boulard's pendulum."

16 ‡ *Red Snow*

A charred beam crashed down and a prickling rush of sparks shot into the air.

"Finding a wooden ball won't return my gold," Paccot said derisively.

James watched the sparks vanish into a sky punctured with fading stars and pulled the string through his fingers. It was waxy and hard from use.

"She uses it to find gold."

Laura fretted with impatience. If only Paccot would move instead of standing so stolidly while his shed burnt and the thief fled down the mountain. She wanted to seize Madame Boulard and tear the collar from her.

"You'll catch her if you hurry," Laura said urgently.

"How do I know it's not one of your stories? She could have dropped it when I saw her the other day."

"We saw her with it yesterday." Laura wanted to shake Paccot.

"I hadn't noticed," James said to no one in particular. "The fog's cleared."

He and Laura could chase the thief down the mountain. Whoever it was had only a few minutes start. If it was Madame Boulard, he could be gentle with her, not batter her into the ground as Paccot would. If it was someone else they could . . . He gave up. He couldn't think that far ahead.

"You *must* go!" Laura insisted.

Paccot took the pendulum from James.

"If I go down the mountain, how do I know I'll catch the thief? Who'll milk the animals?"

He spun around, and as if to resolve his dilemma, hurled the wooden ball and the greasy piece of string into the heart of the fire.

"No. I'll have to stay here."

"Let us go," James said. "It'll be light soon."

Paccot shrugged his shoulders.

"What good can you do? But you can take a message to my wife, tell her to send her brother as quick as she can. Follow the path through the forest. Mine is the first farm you'll come to."

James touched Laura's hand. She was gazing at the fire, not listening to what James and Paccot had been saying.

"Laura," James said, "we must start now."

He saw that her eyes looked enormous in the cobweb light from dawn and from the fire and that they were brimming with tears.

"We'll hurry," he said over his shoulder to Paccot.

As he climbed the bank behind the shed, James looked back. The fire was still burning fiercely. The stones on top of the walls glowed with heat. As he watched, one cracked and fell to the ground. But beyond that useless light there was a pale line edging a green sky. The sun was touching the snowfields on the summit of Mont Blanc. He saw Paccot stoop down and pick up his cat and then stand gazing at the ruin of all his work.

James and Laura went down from the col in silence with the glow from the fire spreading over them like a cloak. They could hardly see where to set their feet. They often stumbled, jarring their legs, making their knees ache. Every so often Laura believed she caught sight of a fugitive hurrying ahead, rushing to take shelter in the forest, but each time it proved to be a trick of the light, or a deeper shadow in the ground.

Her mind was torn by her conviction that Madame Boulard had the collar. She couldn't forget Merta's terror as Tural threw open the door. In her grief Laura thought, *she's dead and I never even saw her face.* For a moment she wished Tural would come from the past and exchange Madame Boulard's life for Merta's, returning the girl and taking the woman.

It was not until they had passed the rock where they had rested on the climb to the col and were about to enter the forest that Laura spoke.

"I was right about Madame Boulard all the time," she said broodingly.

James glanced quickly at his sister. Her face was wan and troubled. *Those people she sees must have lived under a curse,* he thought, *and it's working itself out on her.* James felt the past gathering itself to tear his sister away from him.

"I made a pendulum this morning and held it over the map. It circled over Madame Boulard's house and Matthieu's café."

"Why didn't you tell me, James?" Laura said savagely. "I knew it was her."

"It could have been Matthieu."

"Of course it couldn't. He knows nothing about it."

"Why can't it be Matthieu, or anyone else for that matter?" James angrily pushed his fingers through his hair. "You said it was a man."

"We could have gone to her house this morning and taken it from her. Stopped all this happening."

James did not answer.

He followed Laura into the threatening forest. His muscles were growing stiff. He smacked one aching foot down after the other trying not to think about the pain in his legs.

In the forest everything was still and amazingly peaceful. The darkness under the trees was intense and the path only a narrow gray ribbon constantly extending itself before them. Suddenly Laura stopped. She stood stock still and clutched James's arm as he reached her.

"What's that?" she whispered.

She pointed. Something was lying on the path. It looked sinister in the light seeping through the trees.

They crept forward till it was at their feet. Laura peered down. She was looking at Madame Boulard. Her face was bleached and ghastly, framed in the hood of a ski jacket.

Laura grabbed Madame Boulard's shoulders and shook her.

"Where is it!" she shouted. "What have you done with it!"

She began plucking at Madame Boulard's clothes, searching for the collar, expecting to feel its hard, curved shape.

"Stop that!" James tore at Laura's hands.

Madame Boulard groaned and rolled over on her side.

"Leave her alone," James ordered.

Madame Boulard was trying to sit up. James helped her. She sat on the path and held her head in her hands.

"Why did you take it?" Laura's voice was menacing. "You can't keep them, you don't know what will happen."

Madame Boulard looked up.

"Is that you, Laura? Is James with you?"

"Of course he is," Laura snapped. "Where's my bracelet and Merta's gold collar? I know you took them. James found your pendulum right outside Paccot's shed."

"Please stop, Laura." Madame Boulard put her arms around her knees and let her head fall forward. "You found my pendulum."

"What other proof do we need? You stole the collar and my bracelet. You can't deny it."

Laura lowered over Madame Boulard.

"Help me up, James." Madame Boulard held out her hand and James pulled her to her feet. She leaned on him and spoke to Laura.

"You've become corrupted, Laura. You see nothing but plots against you—first Julian and your mother and now me. Do you want to know why you found me lying on the path? Do you think I lie on paths at three in the morning because it pleases me?"

"Who do you pretend did steal it then?" Laura said unrepentently.

"I don't know what you're babbling about, but I'll tell you why you found me here. Your mother telephoned at ten o'clock. She'd called you and there was no reply. She wanted to tell you that Julian's better. She asked if I'd go up to your house. She was very alarmed. I got out my car and drove up there. I found no lights on, no children, the place unlocked, deserted."

Madame Boulard paused.

"You can imagine what your mother said when I telephoned her at the hospital."

She took her hand from James's shoulder and pushed back her hood. She started rubbing the side of her head.

"I shall have a bruise like an egg," she said.

"Were you hit?" James asked.

"Yes. But let me finish. Your mother said she'd last seen you going toward the river. She was nearly hysterical by then. I drove home and tried to work out where you'd gone. I remembered what you said about your visit to Col Depraz. You seemed unusually interested in Paccot."

James interrupted her. "Julian told us to go there."

"So that was it. Anyway, I decided if you had climbed to the col, Paccot would keep you there because of the fog. He might be surly but he'd look after you. I left home at midnight and had nearly passed through the forest when I heard someone running down the path toward me. I saw a man. He rushed at me, he seemed possessed, and as he passed he hit me. Luckily I was wearing my hood." Madame Boulard leaned forward and stared into Laura's face. "Then you started shaking me, Laura."

"How long ago was that?" James asked quickly.

"Not long, five or ten minutes."

"Then why was the pendulum there?" Laura sounded as if she hadn't believed one word of Madame Boulard's story.

"I left it in my garden after your last lesson. It wasn't there when I came home, anyone could have taken it."

"Who?"

"Whoever broke into Paccot's shed, obviously."

"Do you expect me to believe that?" Laura said coldly.

"I don't care what you believe. We must all go home now."

"We've got to tell Madame Paccot the shed's burned down," James said.

"I pass their farm on my way home, James. I'll tell her." Madame Boulard's voice did not encourage James to argue with her. "You go home and telephone your mother. That's more important than running messages for Paccot."

Madame Boulard turned away as if she never wanted to say another word to Laura.

They followed her. Laura could still not believe Madame Boulard's story. It was so neat, so filled with justifiable adult rebuke for needlessly alarming their mother.

When they came to the landslide, Laura looked up the path to the cave. The colorless light of dawn was stronger, the trees were now distinct shapes. Halfway up the path she saw a white cardboard box.

Laura threw herself up the mountainside. Paccot's soapbox was lying crushed and broken at her feet. For a second she wanted to pick it up and call James and Madame Boulard. Instead she ran on, and pulling herself around the boulder took the last step into the little clearing. It was like stepping into a block of ice.

The bracelet was lying at her feet. The gold seemed to be fading in the thin light of dawn; the modelling on the ears of wheat and face was softening. As she stooped to touch it a wind from the heart of winter surged around her. Sounds were breaking into her head, pushing out everything she knew. She heard the voice of Loen calling from a great distance.

For a moment she hung between the present and the past, then Merta's pain engulfed her. The weight of the collar was pressing cruelly into her throat. The bracelet was a band of fire on her arm. Her hands bound to the saddlebow ached and the cords cut into her ankles with each movement of the horse.

Tural was a black, forbidding shape ahead of her in a night turning to dawn. His horse had drawn level with Flear's. He leaned forward in the saddle to peer at the horseman blocking the path. Harness creaked on the horses ridden by the men Tural had brought with him to sack Loen's hall.

A cry cut through the expectant stillness, swords clashed, a horse skittered on ice and fell screaming. Behind her Loen's men were attacking Tural's, cutting them down.

"Merta!" Loen was calling her.

Tural threw himself off his horse. His knife sliced the ropes binding Merta. The matted hairs on his arm scraped her cheek. She tried to cry out but the pain at her throat was too great. Tural dragged her into the forest. Flear climbed stumbling over the snow like a wounded bird of prey trailing stiff wings.

Tural threw Merta behind a boulder and stood daring her to move. They were on a little shelf cut from the mountainside. She could still hear fighting on the path below. Snow burned her cheek.

A howling wind was tearing at Flear's cloak making it billow around her like tongues of black flame.

Tural looked at his mother. His face was drawn. He was afraid, as if the forest, for so long his ally, cloaking his deeds, had at last turned to strike. Each tree had become a threat, the darkness under them a wave to blot him out.

"Shall I kill her?" His arm moved harshly as he pulled his sword from its scabbard.

Flear smiled at Tural. She held up her arms to the wind as if she was seeking it to carry her away.

"Wait! She has only a few moments left."

Suddenly the wind died. Merta looked up. A dying moon, thin as hair, hung above the trees.

She heard someone racing up the mountain. For an instant Tural stood poised. The sword swung above his head, his voice grated over her like a file. As the sword swept down the air was brushed by a fluttering line. She saw cloth and flesh split as a spear drove into Tural's chest, saw the jarring tremor as it stayed, then the haft dropped, pulling Tural forward.

Tural saw Loen. He tried to raise his sword. His other hand groped before his face. She saw Loen strike, heard the blade smack. Tural's body fell, his head spinning a red trail across the snow to Flear's feet.

Merta shut her eyes, heard the same rending screams which rose up from the snow Flear in Gian's hut. She knew when Flear died. The bracelet slipped down her arm. She snatched it off. She lifted the collar from her neck and threw it on the snow beside the bracelet.

Loen was running toward her, lifting her to her feet, wrapping his arms around her. She was alive.

"There's a cave. I'll bury the collar there."

Loen warily lifted up the collar. He roughly pulled Flear's body aside and disappeared into the mountain. When he came out he threw Tural's sword after the collar and piled stones to block the entrance. Then he jerked the spear from Tural's headless body and picked up the bracelet on its point.

"We must go to the river, Merta."

Just as he was leading her past the boulder, Merta looked around. The sun had nearly risen. The moon had vanished. Flear and Tural sprawled on the snow which melted and steamed. Their heads lay close together, the sightless eyes staring at each other, their pale hair twined into a net on the trampled snow.

Merta looked at the newborn world as she walked down the path. The sky was a pure blue, the snow shone. Loen's horse was waiting on the track.

He lifted her onto the saddle and led the horse down to the river. They reached the gap and paused for a moment watching the river rushing by.

"They killed Sethor and burned your hall," Merta said.

"I saw the flames as I rode back. My last hope was that Flear and Tural would come this way."

Loen swung the spear. The bracelet flew out over the water and fell close to the opposite bank. He dipped the point in the water which flowed red for an instant and then ran clear.

Merta put her hand under Loen's long red hair and touched his neck.

He looked up at her.

Loen's face held for a moment, young, serene, full of love for Merta. Then it faded, vanishing into darkness while the river flowed on.

17 ⚓ *Under the Walnut Trees*

Laura's heart wrenched with loss. She looked at the bracelet Arne had made and knew that however much she
wanted to be with Loen again, it would never let her.

She stood quite still, letting her own time pull her into
itself. She could hear James talking to Madame Boulard,
but there was another sound. A low rustling breath. It
swept over her. She looked around the clearing. The dawn
was breaking and the trees were filling with color. A bird
flew overhead.

The breathing faltered, then came again, each draught
of air tearing the lungs apart. She listened, unable to
move. The pauses between each breath were sometimes so
quick and short, sometimes so agonizingly long she
thought the sound she dreaded would never come. Laura

shivered. She was listening to the struggling, rustling breath of someone dying.

She walked slowly toward the grasping roots of the fallen tree. The interval between each shuddering breath grew longer, each breath as it came more labored. The sound was coming from the entrance to the cave.

Laura looked into the space between the tree and the cave and saw not the heads of Flear and Tural but Matthieu. He must have fallen from the wall of rock above the mouth of the cave and was lying tumbled on his back. His neck was twisted to an angle it was never meant to take. His breath rattled at longer and longer intervals and his eyes stared into a time far behind the moment of Laura watching him. The knuckles of one hand showed hard and bony like white pebbles. The other, sliced with long furrowing scratches made by a cat's claws, held the golden collar to his broken neck.

James touched her arm. Madame Boulard was beside him.

They listened to one last gasping breath and then there was silence. The next night there would be no moon. The spell was broken.

Laura stared at Matthieu's face. In the first light of dawn it was a wan gray like Tural's and Flear's.

"Take the collar, James, I daren't touch it."

James remembered prising the iron from Laura's hand. The gold collar resisted him as he tried to take it. Matthieu's grip still held. James pulled and as the hand released the collar it fell back covering Matthieu's face.

"Let me have that, James."

He had forgotten Madame Boulard as they watched Matthieu die.

James gave her the collar.

"You take the bracelet, Laura. How can it harm you now?"

Laura went to where it lay in the grass.

"Poor Matthieu," Madame Boulard said as Laura picked up the bracelet. "He must have heard what we said in my garden. Nothing had gone right for him lately. We're all too tied up with ourselves."

She drew Laura and James away from Matthieu. The last thing Laura noticed was that Matthieu was dressed in the brown clothes he always wore.

Laura sat with her back against one of the walnut trees. *Poor Matthieu,* she thought.

He had received the customary village funeral, black curtains, edged with silver, hanging outside the church door, the tolling bell. He had no family and was mourned hypocritically by all those who had never visited his café, the strangeness of his death making them walk behind his coffin.

James had taken on Matthieu's cat. At first it had meowed a bit, but soon it grew to like sleeping on James's bed when the sun shone there, and then going upstairs to Julian's to sprawl against his legs while Julian made long telephone calls to Navier. Julian had made Paccot rich.

Laura pulled a long piece of grass and started chewing out the sap. She was beginning to understand Julian. He had listened to her tell him all about the bracelet. She smiled to herself as she recalled her gratitude when he had said again and again how lucky she was to have found something so beautiful. He never suggested selling the bracelet. He said she should treasure it for the rest of her life. Then he described Matthieu coming to him that day when he had been fishing. Matthieu had demanded to know what Julian had to do with Paccot, and when Julian refused to tell him, he had caught hold of Julian, who slipped and hit his head on a rock.

Laura looked at the straggle of woods in the valley. For a moment she wondered if she should get the bracelet and stare into the golden eyes to see if they would take her back to Loen. She remembered that would mean going down to Madame Boulard's house. She had loaned it to her after showing it to Julian some days ago. Now it was no longer a thing of awe and mystery. Matthieu's death seemed to have drained it of all power.

She looked up at the branches shading her from the sun and thought of the horseman who had sheltered under the walnut trees, his outstretched hand imploring her to help him. *Perhaps I did,* she said to herself. She tried to see Loen's face, but she was distracted by the sound of the river coming to her through the noise of James sawing firewood in the barn.

Then quite unexpectedly she remembered three very ordinary things, the old iron chairs outside Matthieu's café, the peach stones lying on the gravel, and the dented cap of a beer bottle.